Born on the Lupercalia - the Roman festival of the wolf - in 1967, Adam Nicke spent an unhappy and lonely childhood in a series of isolated houses along the Welsh Border. During this difficult period he sought refuge in literature and within his imagination.

When he grew up, his artistic tendencies were first expressed in the designing and making of clothing, most notably for Wayne Hussey of The Mission. Later, he turned to writing fiction which explores an inner realm of moods and anxieties, and the feelings of guilt experienced by characters coming to terms with an alienating world. He has a degree in Literary Studies from the University of the West of England.

Adam Nicke Publishing

Reviews left on Amazon or Goodreads help promote the books you love.

Published by Adam Nicke Publishing, 2018
adamnicke@gmail.com

Cover design by Adam Nicke
Imprint: Independently Published

ISBN-13: 978-1729642191 (Paperback)
ISBN-10: 1729642195 (Paperback)

Dedicated to my maternal grandfather, Jack Tagg
1919-2016

The brother shall betray the brother to death, and the father the son; and children shall rise up against their parents, and shall cause them to be put to death ... But he that shall endure unto the end, the same shall be saved.
~ Mark 13:12

Temptation

Temptation

The mind can make
Substance, and people planets of its own
With beings brighter than have been, and give
A breath to forms that can outlive all flesh

Byron

Temptation

As I close my eyes strange and wonderful shapes animate themselves: images from the purple pageantry of the imagination; archetypes from age upon age that have waited, watching from dark and hollow recesses. Shining, divine lights flow like weightless waterfalls: golden and anointing. Could I ever convey the experience with words? Words are the tools of humanity; I walk with gods. Writing of such things as I now see them is almost beyond me, for only now can I see that everything in the universe has always been housed within my body, a body that now stands on the brink of an abyss. Death holds me in its soft and gentle arms. All things living and eternal pulse within and without everything my senses fall upon. Not that there is a 'me' to perceive it all. There was never an 'I'. In vanity, previous thoughts indicated there was something deep within that had constituted identity: that was the real *me*. To realise that all one's identity is founded upon nothing more than an endless stream of thoughts, fears, hopes, and dreams is strangely liberating. There is no 'I' or 'me' to stand outside those shifting sands, at all.

Options seem limitless and infinite, yet death smiles. Ah to die! To drift into unknown realms, where gentle rivers kiss with lips of beatitude. Only now can I feel life; facing death.

It seems obvious to me that those that either will

not, nor cannot, see with my eyes - eyes that now bear witness to the beating of a transfigured heart, a heart of stardust and as old as time - that these few words will be nonsense. Still, I must try, even as the fire of exultation burns within me and my flesh grows weak. It is a sobering experience to think that these hands are capable of murder. All I had ever wanted was to be free - free to choose for myself - yet my every choice had been moulded by others. Their thoughts had always lain cruel dominion over my every action. There could never be a turning away for they had always been there, like an evil virus, drawing strength from weakness. Yet from death came life! Alas, time is short.

My name and the date of my birth are less important than the eldritch tale I have to tell so, without further ado, I shall begin.

I was an only child. My friendship with Sebastian seems to go back to the point when I first felt my loneliness and despair to be unbearable. Prior to that, there had been no-one, other than family. Perhaps he has always been there, a part of me.

My parents' house was considerably larger than any others in the area. The downstairs had large windows that stretched from floor to ceiling, and beautiful on sunny days when the light of Helios shone and chrysanthemum-like rays would shimmer upon the old flagstone floor; on days when the weather was bad, however, the whole house appeared grey and damp, as though a storm might erupt within its confines: my childhood was invariably grey and stormy. The house, it seemed, had always been there with its rough, stone countenance, seemingly drawn from the rocks upon which it sat, giving it the appearance of something naturally occurring. Yet, for all that, it seemed as if it had once been a happy house. The right family - a *happy* family - might well have enjoyed the many gardens it stood amongst; the honeysuckle crowding the back door that made warm summer nights come alive with odours deliciously ageless; children might have enjoyed each dark room filled with dark secrets or the long staircases that seemed to reach from heaven to hell. Blackened beams supported every room. Every night they seemed to wheeze as relentlessly as the old miners in the local village.

Given the isolated and windswept location of my parents' home it is possible that my destiny was always going to be that of a lonely and withdrawn individual, irrespective of later events that ensured such a disposition. Yet even then, in those first years, I had a rare plant that few cultivate: an imagination!

The house had been built in the foothills of one of the giant jagged mountains that are so abundant in Wales. The previous owner had obviously been a keen gardener, but years of neglect had had an effect on the landscape he had sought to perfect. Nature had waited to reclaim her offspring and now the garden retained only a portion of its former order. As a child, that garden seemed to me to be steeped in mystery that unfolded in silent supplication. Everywhere there seemed new delights: an ancient rose garden, thick with perfume and heavy with the loving care with which the unseen hand had once caressed it. On the little gravel paths, covered in moss, I often pondered on how many dead generations had walked those paths, breathed those perfumes and spoken of their lives, loves, hopes and dreams. Huge rolling lawns reached out to winding steps that seemed to lead nowhere. All those forgotten plans that had never come to fruition; or maybe they had: when did one make the appraisal? Perhaps, at some distant point in the past, everything *had* been right. Perhaps everything was still in the ascent and at some future date everything *would* be right, but then how would we ever know when that moment was?

At that time that garden afforded me many a happy reverie. Every plant seemed fluid and sensuous, able to radiate an inner light, a light illuminating the darkest caves of my imagination. Nothing needed contemplation, for it was already understood.

On rainy days the garden offered some little escape from the oppression of the house. I wanted the garden to gently hold me until the sadness fled. On summer days I became heir to the universe for at those times everything seemed right, true, and honest. I knew how the grass felt to wash in the morning dew; how every flower felt to be touched by the sun. Birds resting on the golden boughs above sang for me and all creation. The child, like the generous rose, gave itself without discrimination. Existence was given purpose by the pleasure of giving.

In this garden, however, lurked a serpent. At the far end of those Elysian fields was a gate, almost otherworldly in all its baroque glory. It felt dangerous for beyond it was something terrifying. It repelled me but also captivated me. Its charm appeared hypnotic. Its penetrating form seemed to reach up and lacerate the sky.

Had it been forged to keep me out? Worse still, to keep something in? What terrors lurked beyond it, submerged in that awful gloom? Even daylight seemed reluctant to enter more than a few feet down the steps beyond - that infernal realm – that it guarded so well. In the rare moments' courage could be mustered to look at it, nothing could be seen save for those few steps down, yet where did they lead?

Even today, that long, hot summer comes back to me. That summer the garden became more important in my life than ever. Every day was spent in solitude, creating and peopling planets of my own. Vividly, one day stands apart from the rest. It was a hot day, even for a summer now remembered as searing. Occasional breezes often sped up and down the valley floor punctuating the warmest of days, yet this day was different. This was not a breeze, but a chill so sudden and unexpected it could be likened to an inescapable fall. Unseen hands seemed to throw my body through a sheet of ice, each tiny shard tearing my skin. Petrified fingers clutched my warm heart tightening and constricting with every beat, like an anaconda with its prey. Borne aloft, without control, so cold and hurled toward the gate.

What force threatened to dash the child's brain upon those steely spikes? Then, as quickly as it had all begun, I felt a gentle, graceful lowering until I found myself reclining on the top step, the gate swinging freely open behind me. Previously, the doom and darkness of where those steps lead had frightened me. Now, golden lights spilt forth with love and an amber-like embrace, warm and tender on my prone shape, wrapping me in an everlasting caress.

What was happening? Did *this* sort of thing happen to everyone? Why hadn't the truth been told? I looked out into the garden and everything seemed frozen. What was once green and fertile was now white and sterile. Where had the summer gone? Out there all was cold and numb. Here I had warmth, salvation and a place to call home. Life had beckoned from a hinged egress. Was there never to be a return to what once had been? What to do? To stay? To die? Death comes too easily for it is living that is difficult. Death makes ugly clowns of us all, with no opportunity to redress any calumny heaped upon us, giving us masks where once were faces.

I stood and silently appraised my options. Suddenly, out of the warmth and comfort a cold, deathly hand reached out and clutched at my wrist. Long fingernails, seemingly befouled by an eternity in this subterranean underworld, sank into soft, young flesh. A face drew nearer to my own. The features scared me as they seemed too primitive and savage, like some sort of half-human atavism.

"Come with me," it croaked, the voice rasping like some great beast. I felt a strange compulsion - as though this was my destiny, but then how could that be? How could we ever be free if things were fated? If we never had a choice then why should we feel guilty? Unknowing, uncomprehending, and with the curiosity of a child, I entered.

The gate swung shut behind me. From that moment things would *never* be the same. There could be no going back. I knew the gate would be closed to me, even if I tried its lock. What could one say about my new surroundings? The figure that had pulled me in had, seemingly, disappeared. Now, *anything* seemed possible. Maybe even start a new faith - or kill an old one. Those steps seemed a tunnel to my innermost soul. The first steps had seemed warm and inviting but now, looking down, there was nothing save the absolute blackness of the void. Was that good, or bad? A complete negation but also a complete infinity. An empty canvas where one could paint anything, given the right tools and a vivid imagination.

To touch; to savour every new delight. To feel along rough stone walls. To listen, as each footstep seemed to echo in caverns immeasurable to man. Turning, a passageway had but a single candle to light my way. Unseen hands seemed to guide me. Somewhere, someone - or some *thing* - wanted me to be here. Stumbling toward the little waxen light, the ground beneath me appeared to move. On the dank, dark floor there was to be no salvation. I fell, yet the anticipated pain of my body colliding with hard stone did not cause me to come to a painful halt. Floor and walls seemed to crumble. Now, I was plummeting down into what? Upon what was my body to be dashed? Was I really to end here, smashed to annihilation, deep within the earth and with nothing to mark my ever having been?

After falling for what seemed hours, I took a single step forward and regained my footing as easily as if it had simply been the next step in a leisurely stroll. No pain and no sudden, jarring stop merely a step into the dark and safety. Miles of rock, entombing, yet comforting and embracing. Nothing could hurt again. Time became relative. How long had circumstances been thus? A second? A century? Was it all the dream of an old man thinking of himself as young again; or a young man imagining himself as old? Did it matter? It seemed real so wasn't that enough?

Staircases stretched away in all directions. Some went down, snaking their way into the long, dark night whilst others reached high, to new horizons and beyond. This void had everything! The urge to jump, to let myself fall again to who knows where was tempered by curiosity. Spiralling around and around, down and down, the distant walls closed in on themselves.

Ropes, pulleys, chains, all moving as though either powering or being powered, by some mighty engine. Oh, to be king of all one perceives! Without my presence *none* of this mechanism would be in motion, of that I was sure.

Stone faces formed in the walls surrounding me, some smiling, some mocking; some mournfully sad, others hysterically laughing; death masques showing the whole panoply of human emotion yet one thing united them all: they were all of the same countenance, the face now known to me as Sebastian. Stone eyes followed my every move.

If only the workings of this place could be remembered! If my presence was the essential component, it had to be important to retain something of this mechanism. Herein lay the secret to everything but everything retained a breath of the arcane that made their workings as elusive as the philosopher's stone. Fleeting glimpses of the magnitude of it all dissolved as quickly as the reflection of Narcissus in a pool, but then how fleeting was fleeting? A second? A century?

Wheels continued to spin and grind as the whole machine trundled along, endeavouring to perform some unfathomable and distant task, perhaps since the beginning of time and perhaps until the end. Perhaps that was the way of things. Stone eyes still watched. Watching for a mistake? What if a mistake were made? What were the rules? Did I make the rules? If I were now making the rules then how could I *ever* make a mistake? Maybe the rules were always changing so they could never be known. If only those petrified eyes would stop staring...

Would it ever be possible to leave this place? To be a child again in the garden! Now there was no way to go, only down. Down to what? Down there was unknown. Down there it was cold, so very cold. Even thinking about it brought chill winds blasting, as cold as the icy hand that had brought me to this place. What to do?

Walking with trepidation, and on weary legs, flesh became stone. Was there really no escape from this tomb? No, there *had* to be a way out of this place. Suddenly, I was back in the garden with the sun shining. It seemed a nice day. I let out a deep breath and lay back in the grass so that the warm rays of the sun could vivify me a little. I must have fallen asleep, I figured, and had a dream. I tried to rationalise it. How could something I

Temptation

had always feared have become dangerous and exciting? I had tasted freedom and wanted more. It wasn't just the gate in the garden I had opened but another gate in my heart; one that could never more be closed. That dream had been a rite of passage. I may not have realised it then but I realise it now. I was breaking away from the life I had known and that day was the start of life anew.

If the reader will permit me, scant attention needs to be accorded to my school years; my time is short and if I am to commit to paper all that needs to be recorded, these last few hours can be better spent than recollecting such tedious events. I have to execute some discernment and I choose to edit this portion of the story.

Suffice to say my school days were, largely, unhappy. Fortunately, they had no detrimental effect on my education. Initially, these years were uneventful. Geographical isolation had made me unsociable even though I longed to be otherwise. In fact, the only friend throughout those years was Sebastian.

Sebastian was a quiet boy. Even though we were inseparable he always remained a little unknown to me. He seemed to keep so much to himself. He never spoke of his family, his home life, where he lived, or where he had been. He seemed to have come from nowhere and simply existed.

Vividly, I remember one visit Sebastian paid me.

Temptation

My father didn't even give him a glance but it was the conversation afterwards that I recall. By this time, I hated being anywhere near my father and felt acutely self-conscious that his personality should show itself to anyone outside of the family. My mother and I enabled the tyrant rather than expose him for the bully that he was. I had already realised that I had to break the chains of familial paternity were I ever to be free.

Unlocking the heavy back door, the twilight sun shone through the cascade of honeysuckle that sensuously encircled the door frame so that the whole air seemed alive with life.

"God, what an atmosphere! I can see why you're like you are. His piety can go to hell", Sebastian said.

"Be quiet, will you! He'll hear you."

"All that religious nonsense on the bookshelves. It doesn't fool me."

"Well, he is a Christian," I countered.

"Christianity! Don't start me on that!"

"Don't you believe in God, then?"

"Do you believe in Santa Claus?"

"Of course not."

"Well, there's your answer."

"Haven't you ever asked yourself why we are here, or where we are going?"

"Yes, I have." By now, we had descended the broken stone steps and had found our way onto one of the lawns.

Temptation

"And?"

"And what?" He was well aware that I wished him to continue yet would not do so until I asked.

"Do you? What conclusion have you come to?" I asked.

"That I want more from Christianity than it actually gives. I don't want a religion that makes me feel guilty for something I haven't done. I don't want a religion that puts another man to death to save me. That's awful. Why are we taught to believe superstitions as if they are demonstrable fact? And what about the people the church venerates? I know your father beats your mother, you know. Christianity is misogynistic so no wonder he approves! Tertullian said of women 'thou art the Devil's gate'. St. Jerome that 'woman is the root of all evil'. St. Augustine asked 'why was woman created at all'. Odun of Cluny even asked who would wish to hold 'ipsum stercoris saccum' and that loosely translates as 'a stinking bag of dung'. Ask your mother what she thinks such a religion can offer her! If these are the people a Christian church looks up to, then it is a church I can do without. The Christian concept of God is dead. Look inside yourself and ask 'What do I think of such and such as a person?' not 'What do I think of such and such as a Christian?'"

We turned left, our boot heels crunching on the narrow gravel path and on to one of the lawns, where we sat.

Temptation

"What is it you want, then?" My manner was rather truculent. After all, being brought up to believe in the biblical account of creation, I now found myself listening to a friend voicing every doubt I had begun to harbour about the faith in which I had so long believed. Was my castle *really* built on sand?

"I want to escape. I dream of the past, and the future - of other times, other places and exotic lands! Of great heights where the picturesque becomes the sublime. A place where everything I know now might be left behind! Of mountains where I can see forever. But what is life if not an existence that is chaotic and confusing? Does anyone want a life that has no hope or reason? Do not tell me it is because I am an unbeliever. It is because I was once a believer that I now feel so betrayed. I don't want rational explanations, I want mystery, not mystery presented as fact. I want to live in a world where *anything* is possible. I'm supposed to be free yet everywhere I am in chains. Sometimes it feels as though I'm swimming in a bottomless ocean of treacle and with every new stroke, I sink further and further away from the cool morning. All I have are my moods and the ceaseless ebb and flow of my thoughts and they're all that constitutes *me*. I want to find others like me, for, like you, all that ever spoke to me before was God but God is a liar. I grew up and stepped out of the nursery and now face maturity without such a crutch." With that, he paused and picking up a broken branch that lay nearby idly flicked at the grass.

"I once read of a man who, when looking at the night sky, felt a dual awe. On the one hand, he witnessed the infinity of starry space, on the other, the inner workings of himself. I want to synthesize the two - infinity without and infinity within. Before I fall asleep it sometimes comes to me - when everything is dark and hidden - the powers that drive the universe come and unfold their secrets and I see the majesty of it all. At that moment *anything* seems possible. Each star could be ten, with every planet around each star the home of someone as lonely as me, none of us ever complete without the other. I want all those lonely people by my side, so I too may feel the warmth of human affection. Do you understand?"

"I think so," I mumbled. I did, of course, but it felt blasphemous to say so.

"I feel sure that some veil obscures an entrance to the untapped reservoirs of the mind. Rend that aside and infinity will rain down upon us like a summer shower on a hot July day," he continued before suddenly stopping. I looked at him for some explanation, in time to see him frown. The silence continued for what seemed like an age until be drawled "I never want you to repeat this. If you speak of it and you shall not see me again." It was easy to see the look of cold earnestness in his face: I could tell that he meant what he said, yet felt angry that he thought such a threat was needed and that his friendship meant so very much to me. What did he think I would do without him? Wither and die? Who was *he* to think that withholding his friendship would be a punishment? Another part of me, however, wanted to hear what else he had to say, so I bid him continue by nodding my acquiescence. He was about to continue when the sound of a door being slammed interrupted us. A few light steps scurried upon the path that led to the garden, before a face as familiar as my own came into view.

"You're not going to be able to come back in at the moment," said my mother, as she approached. She looked furtively at Sebastian, clearly wishing to conceal the real reason for our exclusion.

"I'll open the side door for you. If you can stay there, there's a good boy." I, of course, knew the real reason why we couldn't return via the door we had left: my father had evidently taken umbrage at what he felt to be some transgression and was now in some sort of rage. I would probably be hit, my mother thrown into a wall or door and who knows what else. That is why we had so few visitors: my mother discouraged them through a sense of shame and humiliation. She would blame herself; ask what her neighbours would think of a woman who could not look after her own home, never realising she was entirely blameless.

The three of us seemed to stay together for a long time, long enough for me to catch a tear trickle down my mother's face. She raised her hand to her eye and wiped the little course away. She smiled and, just for a moment, looked at Sebastian, then back to me with an expression that begged me not to betray her secret - *our* secret. She was a beautiful woman, but most sons probably think that of their mothers. She had grace, poise, elegance and deserved so much more from life.

"I'll go and open it for you." I had quite forgotten the door, being lost in a reverie. There was no hypocrisy in her thinking, only the false virtues of shame and guilt. Before I could reply she had turned away leaving nothing but the warm fragrance of her perfume, and something less tangible and unique: the scent of *my* mother.

"He's made her cry." Sebastian's voice shattered the quiet like a stone dropped into the still waters of a long-forgotten well. It wasn't that he had broken the silence, it was that he had realised *our* secret. His tone suggested that *every* door of that closed and awful world had now been shown to him. My cheeks burned with shame, not just for me, but also for my mother. I wanted to protect her. At that moment, for the first time, I wanted to kill my father.

"Don't be stupid. Why should she be doing that?" I looked at Sebastian. His face softened into the same appealing look my mother had given me. He wanted me to tell him the truth but was sensitive enough not to insist he was right.

Temptation

"Sorry, my mistake." I looked at Sebastian for a trace of sarcasm that his voice had not betrayed yet there was none. He smiled, sensitively. "Now, where's this door?" His voice had changed, his manner now cheery as though he were trying to lift me out of my torpor.

Without looking at him, I turned and led the way around the side of the old house to what would once have been servants' quarters, those occupants now being long gone. Mother and I did any chores that needed doing, whilst a local man came to tend the garden occasionally. We walked to the heavy age-blackened door, recessed a few feet or so into the walls of the house, the walls of the house thus serving as a porch. Either side of the door were two old benches. I gestured Sebastian to sit.

"We'd better take off our boots." It wasn't that carpets would get damaged, for there were no carpets only flagstones of the sort that so many houses of antiquity in Wales have as flooring; my fear was that our heavy boots would make a noise as we walked upon those stones, thus giving away our hiding place.

"May I go in?" Sebastian had removed his boots and stood with his hand on the door handle, his gaze focussing on my attempts to remove my footwear.

"Yes, of course, only be quiet." For added effect, I had whispered the last two words as if the words alone were not enough and had to be demonstrated. How embarrassing, I thought. Why had I done that?

Temptation

By now, the setting sun had almost given way to the silver denizens of the night. Now, a mist from outside had entered, uninvited, and had begun to coil along the ground like some serpentine shroud. Where Sebastian had led, I followed.

"Sebastian." I might as well have spoken, given the volume of my hoarse whisper. There was no reply. By now, the mist from outside had not only begun to make its way into the little vestibule into which the door had led but was now silently making its way up the staircases. There was no sign of Sebastian. The ancient stone floor felt as cold as a corpse beneath my feet. This part of the house was almost unknown to me. It was less the rural estate in which we usually lived and more a country retreat. Strange paintings looked down from the walls, strange in that they were supposed to be of my forebears. Was I really the culmination of that near-extinct, effete lineage? Had people *ever* really looked like that? Where were their eyelashes? Why the pursed lips? Yes, they were strange: otherworldly. There was a creak on a staircase behind me. Stepping through the mist came my friend. He had, evidently, somewhere removed his jacket. Now his white shirt billowed in the gliding motion of his descent. From somewhere he had found a candelabra, in which burned three slender candles. As the rounded staircase brought him a full quarter-circle, he finally faced me. Behind him, light from the night sky swathed his silhouette in translucent darts. Haloed, knee-deep in a carpet of diaphanous, swirling gossamer, he seemed unreal: a phantom of the night.

"Let's have a look around, shall we?" It seems strange to admit that the experience was as much a revelation for me as it was for him. The house was *too* big. This wing I had, maybe, been to once in the last five years. Silently our stockinged feet ascended the stairs. "All these rooms!" It might have impressed some but I think with him it was just a casual observation. He looked at me for a reply but I had none to give.

"How about here?" Sebastian's swarthy fingers took hold of the heavy brass handle and twisted. The door creaked open. He turned to me and, gesturing with his head, beckoned me to follow. The room was neither small nor large, being rather nondescript. At the far end of the room there were a low set of leaded windows, in the Elizabethan manner, that stretched the entire breadth of the wall but a little too low for either Sebastian or myself to look through without bending to do so. Were people ever really that short? In front of the window, and also running the length of the wall, a windowsill large enough to sit upon.

"These bloody candles." I hadn't realised that the flames of Sebastian's candelabra had died. The room seemed well lit but, now that he had drawn my attention to it, it was obvious that all the light in the room came from outside. I walked to the window. By the light of the encroaching night, the whole garden seemed eerie. Multi-hued colours were all becoming the same smoky-blue, punctuated by unknown black shadows. I turned and looked back to Sebastian, who, by now, had placed the candles on the floor and, with his back to me, was endeavouring to light them. My eyes had become accustomed to the brighter light of the garden; by comparison, the room now seemed dark. Looking to the walls, against the ageing whitewash, boxes appeared to be stacked. On the walls themselves, black frames hanging dark pictures. In the gloom, they might have been prints of anything. I looked back to Sebastian, who, by now, had managed to light one of the candles. Standing, he turned.

"We can light the other two from this one." He strode toward me, his attention focused on the job he had set himself. By the time he had reached the window, all three were lit. "Look at that breeze!" I looked at the little flames as he placed them in the window. Far from burning upwards, a chill from the window caused the flame to ripple and splutter at right angles to the wax. "Let's have a look in these boxes, shall we?"

Our eyes soon became accustomed to the dim shadows around the room. Sebastian's attention was captured by a large coffer. Bands of black iron hammered securely into all four sides, in two continuous strips, save for the lid, which was hinged and shut securely with a battered lock. Both Sebastian and I took a few steps toward it, he to the front, I behind.

"Shall we take a look?" I nodded my agreement. The prospect that something secret, something which had lain awaiting rediscovery for so long, was about to be unearthed was made me shiver.

Sebastian kneeled in front of the mighty casket and inspected the lock. Taking it in his fingers he gave it a twist. Rusting metal against rusting metal made a sound that made me wince and him reconsider his plan of approach.

"I'd give it a kick," he said, rising to his feet, "but not without my boots. I'll get something with which I can knock it."

"There look, pass me that gun."

"Gun?" I hadn't noticed a gun. A gun here?

"Yes, behind you." My attention followed the aim of Sebastian's outstretched finger.

"Why is there a gun here?"

"Oh look, does it really matter? I only want something heavy. Pass it to me, will you?" His tone was becoming exasperated. I handed him the gun.

"Make sure it's not loaded."

"Stand back," he said, ignorant of my concern. With a single deft motion, he brought the butt of the gun down upon the padlock. In an instant, it lay broken on the floor. Sebastian handed me back the weapon. "Now then, let's have a look."

Sebastian bent over, clasped the lid where the

iron bands were hammered and lifted. The rusting hinges made a creak as they submitted to the force. Removing one hand to rummage inside, he began pulling at something.

"What is it?" The lid obscured my view: whatever it was, it looked shapeless and ragged.

"I don't know. I think it's an animal skin."

"Oh no!" I made no attempt to disguise the sadness in my voice.

"I said I don't know. Pass me a light so I can see a little better." He nodded his head toward the window. By now, the clear moonlit sky had dark and ominous shapes congregating upon it. As I approached the window, I noticed the rain was now splashing against the glass.

"I think there's a storm coming." I was thinking out loud, trying to distract myself. I was about to turn when something caught my attention. There, in the glass - just for a moment - a face had been looking in at me. In the darkness, it had been indistinct, yet there had definitely been *something*. A flash of lightning lashed across the sky. For a moment - a hideous moment - the whole of the room behind me had been reflected in the wet, leaded glass. In that brief instance I could have sworn I saw Sebastian's face transform into that of a wolf, its gaze never distracted from me as he paced the room.

"Sebastian!" I took a step backwards and fell

taking the candelabra and candles with me. They tumbled to the floor, the molten wax extinguishing the flame. Worst of all, it left us in total darkness.

"Oh, that's just wonderful." My friend made no attempt to hide the irritation in his voice.

"No, you don't understand. In the window ... I saw you turn into a wolf."

"Really? Well, as Acts twenty, twenty-nine says, 'grievous wolves enter in among you'."

"No, I saw it I swear." Already I had the feeling that he didn't believe me.

"I really think your imagination is playing tricks on you, you know," he said, smiling. "Now I'll have to try and light the candles again."

Sebastian had already forgotten my alarm. I rose to my feet and took a few steps toward the window. As I did so, the moon tore away her veil and shot arrows of pale pearlescence upon the whole of the garden beneath. Had there really been a wolf in the room? As I looked from the window, a large canid form moved with stealth across the garden before suddenly scurrying toward the gate as though it were about to launch an attack on some defenceless prey. As I watched, the form reached the sill of the mighty portal and disappeared beyond. Behind me, muttering, Sebastian struggled with the candles. Dare I tell him what I had seen? This time I chose to keep quiet.

"Let there be light."

"And there was light! Thank you, Lightbringer" Once again, the room relaxed under the golden flickering of the candles.

"Now, let's see what this is." I had quite forgotten the chest. Sebastian began to pull what was left of its contents out and on to the floor. Initially, the shape seemed indistinct but as Sebastian began to smooth out the many folds, we both recognised what it was at the same moment.

"Oh no!" Sebastian said as he dropped what he was holding and sat back. On the floor of that high and dusty room, the skin of a white hart, complete with antlers, lay flat and lifeless. "That is just awful. This breaks my heart. Who would want to kill such a beautiful animal?"

With a movement that was frightening in its suddenness, Sebastian leapt to his feet, took hold of the gun he had used to shatter the lock of the chest, and ran to the window. Without a pause, the butt of the shotgun smashed its way through the glass, before being turned and fired. A roar bellowed across the silent night. Through what remained of the window a cold gust of air, like death on a summer night, entered. The gunfire disturbed a family of crows that had thought their day over and who now left the safety of their black trees and ascended the night sky like ebonised angels.

"Bastard!' He shouted. "You bastard."

In an ever-speedier vortex, the wind began to

howl and swirl. Eventually, he leaned forward and rested his hands on the sill beneath the window.

"What's beyond that gate?" he asked. I shrugged my shoulders. "You haven't the courage to look, have you?"

"What do you mean?"

"You know what I mean."

I did know what he meant. There, locked away it was the part of me that was primitive and instinctive. I didn't like it that *he* knew. My upbringing had made unnaturalness seem natural; I could no longer rationalise anything. Everything was sick, affected, decadent and dying. How did he know? Then the thought of that day, years before, when I had had that strange dream and found myself carried through that gate and the journey I had taken beyond it. Was it a madness of my mine to think that my friend had been the man I had met in that place? If that gate - and what lay beyond - was a construct of my own wild imagination then how could it have been peopled with a real-life person? It couldn't, could it?

We faced each other for what seemed like an eternity.

Next day, Sebastian had gone. Later, my father took me aside. His face reddened as he spoke, his tone angrier than it had ever been. His ignoble features bent toward my own. He could never placate or explain, only bully.

Temptation

"I have made arrangements for you to finish your education at a new school. You start tomorrow." That was it. I knew not to ask why, or for what reason, as it would not get a response, only a beating. My only explanation would be because it was what *he* wanted. I had to convince myself it was for the best. Maybe it would give me a chance to become independent. Maybe if I could leave Sebastian's influence behind then things might be different. Now the decision had been taken for me, I had to tell myself that everything would be easier.

The rest of that day was spent in idle contemplation. Occasional glimpses of the gate brought a strange feeling of awakening. I was aware that in stepping from the garden and, once more, through that gate again might well precipitate the end of everything that had given me an identity. Nonetheless, forbidden fruit is often the most tantalising. It was now hung in vine leaves that bore plump, full grapes, whilst a young quince tree made concerted efforts to establish itself a few short feet away. The gate itself looked almost otherworldly; ethereal, as though all that separated me from complete union with all things natural was its foliage. Some invisible and intoxicating ether seemed to connect me directly to it, floating, iridescent and - if I closed my eyes - like tiny rainbows, exploding worlds, or precious gems bursting into flames. It spoke to me with a sobbing voice but it was then that I remembered my friend.

Temptation

I thought on my condition that day. Perhaps it *was* time to cast aside childish thoughts now that I stood on the threshold of maturity, but everything seemed so daunting and invasive. For the first time I really understood - and with all my heart - what Sebastian had felt when he had spoken to me of religion and what he wanted from it. I too longed for infinity, for the transcendent, for something to take me out of my squalid insignificance. My garden no longer supplied the escape that it once had. I had to acknowledge that the gate - that portal to another realm - now had more allure than ever.

That night I lay awake, thinking. My bedside lamp flickering; shadows played, danced, and jumped across the walls like nymphs and satyrs. Lying there, something transfigured the uncertainties of the day. If only I could breathe the lotus flower, or wash in the waters of the Lethe. Why *had* I avoided the gate and the change it might wreak upon me? Maybe it was a symbol, and a symbol of the transition within me that caused me such uncertainty. If I could welcome that transition then with a few brave steps, both literally and figuratively, I could be free. Blissful thoughts of freedom floated in timeless suspension. For a moment, I felt unbounded joy as thoughts gently rippled in fluid formlessness across my inner eye. Dancing with the shadows, I was a shadow; flickering with the flame, I was a flame. A part of everything as everything was a part of me. No past;

no future; only the eternal *now*. White, sterile walls began changing and transforming. Lachrymose autumn tones flooded the room in holy copulation. All manner of artefacts from my dressing table fell to the floor, as though swept aside by an unseen hand. Something life-giving had entered my room. Beating angel wings lifted my curtains so that the heavy fabric seemed to shake in anticipation. Then, a face in the night. With a shatter, the large windows opened. White walls began turning crimson as a sphere of light entered, radiating a spectrum of colours around my small room. From the depths, a figure swirled and gyrated sinuously and sensuously. Drones, like chants intoned in a medieval monastery, seemed to herald a fanfare to my goddess. Thick plumes of incense swirled and clouded, heavy skeins coiling snake-like over everything they gently touched. Slowly, the music ground on as she moved with the same slow eroticism as the feathers of perfume around her. Her lithe, tanned body - the colour of ancient cinnamon from some far distant spice trail - adorned in decoration as exquisite as the form upon which they rested. Silver; gold; gem upon gem framed and accentuated her perfect symmetry. Every beautiful facet of those precious stones seemed to compliment and extol the aspect of their peers. Then the face! Lips as red as a wound; eyes blacker than a sinner's soul; skin as taut as the sinews of my heart - a heart which looked, and died - upon such perfection! Even the tresses of hair framed the most perfect of portraits. Come closer, my lady without mercy! Each century of her moving brought pain and pleasure. Ah, to touch! Suddenly, each thin layer of fabric that covered me was torn aside in a movement unseen. Cool hands on hot, damp skin.

"Who are you?" I mumbled incoherently, every fractured nerve longing for her lacerating caress.

"I am Lillith. I am Salome. I am the spirit of Sodom," she breathlessly intoned, her lips running a burning course upon my moist skin. Bared teeth sank into my soft neck, painlessly opening a vein. I closed my eyes in ecstasy as my lifeblood spurted forth into her eager mouth, besmearing lips in crimson stains. Only the agitated, irregular fluttering of my heart - like the beating wings of an eagle in a gilded canary cage - came to my ears. Then, the low murmur of delight: the deep, guttural groan of her consummated desire. A new, strange consciousness swept over me as my angel of the pit began to lick, like a wild beast with its new offspring. Beneath that mouth, my ethereal form stirred. In an instant, all that connected an eternal part of me to the temporal prison of the flesh was a shimmering silver thread, like a cool brook on a summer's day.

"Sebastian." Her heavy-lidded, satisfied eyes could barely open as her stained lips shaped the whispered words.

"No, I'm not Sebastian," I replied in stupefied and distant confusion.

Temptation

"Sebastian," again her soft breath brushed my naked skin. "Sebastian." Floating; hypnotising.

"Is this death? Am I dead?"

"Not dead, but dreaming," she murmured as she drew her nails down my chest. Pathways of light now reached from my room to the horizon. Out, over the garden; out, over the trees, valleys, mountains: a pathway safe and eternal. Onward we went, high above towns and cities. Over measureless expanses of purple-black water shimmering in mercury night. Onward, ever onward, to a dark wood. There, a flame consumed the still and silent night. There, too, we stopped: where earth joined air; air joined fire; fire met water, we spiralled to the ground.

In the distance, an elevated platform supported a throne, yet in the blackness, nothing seemed to stir: sublime space! My companion placed her finger to my lips and pursing her own mouth gestured for my silence. An unearthly quietness followed broken only by a distant, thunderous procession. A thousand pounding cloven hooves presaged dark and fearful shapes appearing out of the gloom with what, I felt, were all-seeing eyes. Horned gods, antlered and as wild as stags. Sinuous forms like panthers, leopards. Great animals pulling chariots adorned with leaves from this sylvan glade. Strange beasts emerged; men and women carousing in ecstasy. Then, the great god enthroned with syrinx and crook clutched close. Dust turned to fertile earth. Couples raced naked to cool waters: anointing and baptizing the earth in holy copulations. I speak of joy and holy communions! Bodies; flames; naked skin glistening, inflamed by fire; desire. Dancers whirled in circles, shrieking and laughing. In the midst, turning, the great beast had features known to me: Sebastian!

What had gone so terribly wrong as a child when communion with nature had been as natural as breathing? Like an empty vessel, had I turned to Sebastian for succour? He was nature whilst I was ... something wrong. To be loved only drew my suspicions for what was there to love? I could only return love with hostility, testing the other's affections and bitterly congratulating myself when I had succeeded in turning love to hate. To love would be to allow a thawing of what lay within and to give away a deep and secret thing; what if that were then rejected? How could I ever communicate the *real* me, anyhow? People only like others for the feelings they elicit within *them*. Love is always a selfish act, even if we like to think otherwise. People might listen, but how many are really interested? Sebastian had been right to think the transcendent an incommunicable thing. What about my unique experience? Always it would tinge the happiest of experiences with hues of melancholia.

I awoke with a jolt. My light had gone, not that that mattered anymore. The first rays of the morning had joined in majestic union with the earth, lighting the room in a coy brilliance. I arose, strode to the door and opened it. A brief look back confirmed what I had been thinking: the room, if nothing else, was as it had always been.

Thinking of the night before was difficult. Surely it had all been a phantasmagorical flight of fancy? Now, in the penetrating light of day, it all seemed so vague. Perhaps it was better for it to remain that way. Ah, bittersweet memories! What was the past? An intangible breath that only supplied phantoms to haunt the present. My memories were of no importance to anyone except me. For good or bad they were, nonetheless, unique. What, after all, did any of us have? A dead past; a future that never comes; a present that is instant history. All I had was myself, and how fragile that was! All truth could ever be was what I wanted it to be because my truth might be a lie to another. That day I took a step into the unknown, away from Christian absolutes, away from what other people wanted me to be. It was a difficult, stumbling step, for one harsh word from another would always cause me to tumble. In order to make the rules, one needed to play the game yet, often, I felt too hidebound to even participate.

I made my way to the kitchen. I knew my father would have already left, so at least my mother and I would be able to talk in peace. I opened the door. There, at the far end of the room stood that cherished frame: she whom I adored. I had thought my bare feet to be silent on the old stone floor as I approached, but that notion was soon dispelled,

"Morning, dear." She busied herself at the old porcelain sink, lifting a hand to crank the water pump that, even then, must have been a hundred years old. Finally, she turned. A dark shade on her cheek spoke volumes. Ought I to mention it? The closeness of our bond made the silence all the more awkward. Trying to look anywhere save the hideous bruise upon her delicate face my eyes were, nonetheless, drawn to that place and no other.

"I hit it on a door this morning." Already she had guessed what I was thinking, or maybe her own sensitivity to the disfigurement wished to draw my attention to it before she thought I had noticed.

"Did you?" It was painful to see how she felt it necessary to lie, even to me. Did she think she was protecting me? Protecting her husband? Guilt had fastened itself to our family like a horrible tumour. There was a long pause.

"No, you know I didn't, don't you?" I raised my eyes from the floor to meet her gaze. There could be no more untruths. However painful the experiences, she and I bore them *together* - a partnership forged in suffering. We had the mother and son relationship, but more than that we were now allies fighting a common enemy. What if she still did still love him? It was more a love for what he once was rather than the person he had become, I was sure. I hated him for the way he had taken her love and thrown it to one side as though it were something worthless. What could I now say?

"Yes, I know. I've always known." The words weren't that comforting, but such a situation often makes the right words difficult ones.

"Have you?" There didn't seem any hint of a surprise in her response. Maybe his success had been that all her responses were now flat, dead, ones. "I'm so sorry."

"Sorry for what?" It seemed incredible that, despite it all, she still blamed herself.

"I didn't want it to be like this." She, too, seemed to be struggling for the right words to say. Her brow knitted. Her eyes closed, yet tears still began running down her face. "I wanted to give you a good life. I wanted you to be happy. He wasn't always like this. He was a good man … once."

"We can't go on like this." I tried to imagine her desperation. I felt trapped but knew one day I would be able to leave, whereas her life must have felt like an eternal punishment. Her only option was to stay and hope he would change, meanwhile suffering the bullying and tyranny that had come to constitute their marriage.

"I can't imagine my life without him. I still love him." This time the tears came in floods. Turning away from me she bent over the kitchen sink and sobbed.

Temptation

What could I do? After all, I had to leave that day. How could I leave a situation, like this? Did that man realise what he was doing to the both of us? Did he even care? For a moment I turned away. The sight of my mother, crushed, was just too pitiful. My attention came to rest on the door that, moments earlier, had hastened my entrance. There was that dent in it. I must have been about ten years of age when I saw him pull her by the arm, swinging her into it, then his concern for the damaged door.

"You must do something." I turned to face her. Already she had composed herself and was wiping the tears away on a little white handkerchief.

"I'll be alright. You go to your new school and enjoy yourself. When you come home again everything will be alright, you'll see." I don't think she believed the words but, for her sake, I mustered a smile. I had intended to bewail my own misfortune at having to attend a new school. Now, my pain seemed insignificant. I felt guilty. Looking at her, she seemed different. For the first time, she had become more than just a mother. She was unique - a person with the same dreams, hopes, ambitions, and loves, as anyone else. Why should she be denied the right to love, and be loved, by someone who could feel no-one's suffering but his own? My mother was beautiful, yet blighted by tragedy. Something, somewhere, had gone horribly wrong for her, yet she bore it all with dignity. Her blue eyes as deep as an ocean looked at me with pride. All her dreams were invested in me. If I let myself down, then I would be letting *her* down.

"Do you think it will be a good school?" I tried to change the subject, to speak of lighter things and to lift her spirits a little, so that she might dream it a wonderful place: a place where her son could be happy, his happiness, in turn, bringing happiness to her.

"I'm sure it will." A light came from deep within her eyes and a smile stole over her face.

A little while later, after a final preparation, a little time was left to kill before the carriage would come to take me away from this place. The last days of summer made everything appear elegantly decayed. Yes, everything *would* be alright because it *had* to be. It may have been an argument, I had told myself a hundred times, yet each time the statement seemed more and more absurd. Perhaps everything *was* as it should be. Perhaps everything was right because it had been ordained that way. But then how could that be? How could any god see the torment being meted out on this good woman and stand by and do nothing?

Without realising, my wanderings around the garden had led me to the gate. It no longer seemed terrifying. Now, it appeared benevolent and kind. Nonetheless, something made me stop. To go any further would be to confront something that, from my earliest days, I had denied. Dare I embrace something that unknown, dark, and unfettered? There were serpents in my garden. Only on the distant horizons were there waterfalls drenching all creation in a rich ablution, washing life into the inanimate. Out there - somewhere - was freedom; salvation. People passed: I stood among them, but not of them; in a shroud of thoughts which were not their thoughts. To sleep; to die; to break these chains of convention.

Later that day I started my new school. My experiences there were painful ones so I shall not dwell, to any great degree, on my time there. The regime there was very different from my previous school. Even the building was markedly different, in every respect. My old school had once been a nunnery, converted into a seat of learning after the decline of Catholicism in Wales. The building itself had been splendid in its gothic pretensions: corridor upon corridor that seemed to lead to nowhere; dank, dark passages which, in my naiveté, I believed might well have led to hell.

My new school was just a few miles from the old one, but might as well have been a few thousand. One might have supposed that it would have had the same ambience of religious degeneration as the old school given that it was once an old rectory. There, however, the similarity ended.

My tutor - Mr Torquemada - seemed intent on making my days there as unbearable as possible. Discipline was harsh and executed with zeal but always, of course, under the aegis of piety. To him, pleasure was a sin. In retrospect, every sentence that the man uttered stank of control cloaked as Christian morality. Even subjects I had previously enjoyed became painful as the self-righteous Mr Torquemada sought to impose his will upon mine. He was the mortar and Christianity the pestle, whilst I - the grain - was ground to dust between the two.

A solitary light burned in the darkness: Lillian. She was another pupil at the school, yet she was different. A part of me moved with her. In her free, easy manner, elements of Sebastian evinced themselves. She moved with grace, dignity, and deportment. She, unlike myself, appeared proud of the person that she was. I longed to talk to her but how could I muster the courage when I knew I could do nothing for her?

That academic year passed with dismal slowness. By attrition, Mr Torquemada finally succeeded in suppressing all that was natural within me yet all the while Lillian inflamed such natural desires, leaving me feeling both guilty and disgusted.

By the end of that year, my love for Lillian was boundless and immeasurable. Every part of me wanted to be a part of her. It's true to say that I would have died for her.

Nonetheless, a pitiless sun beat upon my sole oasis; a serpent that fastened itself into every part of me. Being so tightly bound by artifice, there, at last, came a point of no return. I had left something raw and essential behind so long ago that, at times, it seemed to have never been there at all.

By June, my school days were nearing completion and my sense of doom had increased tenfold. All around me life, as I thought it was meant to be lived, was in decay; putrefying bodies of joy. Why? With the bony hand of self-doubt upon my shoulder, feelings magnified in the presence of my father. My head spun in turmoil as I thought of things and with no release, I began physically hurting myself so that my mental anguish had some release. It started with needles but progressed to nicking my arms with a cut-throat razor. It wasn't healthy - I knew that - yet seeing the blood flow down my arm and spill into a white porcelain sink felt like a release. If only Sebastian and I had still been friends. I missed him. His company was timeless: fresh. He was everything I aspired to be but was told to abhor. Many things had changed since we last met: Mr Torquemada, father, Christianity and the patriarchal system, it seemed, had given me an identity. However miserable life was, I was told, death would bring its just rewards.

On the last day of term, the shapeless spirituality that had been floating inside me, at last, seemed to coalesce into a very definite shape. As I sat in the dusty classroom listening to Mr Torquemada's final lesson - on how physical pleasure had been sent by the Devil and that we must all seek to rise to a more spiritual plane - it dawned on me how I could escape *all* temptations. By taking up the cloth, how could evil ever tempt me again? If putting aside hedonistic pursuits for a life of quiet prayer was the only way it could be done, then so be it.

I left school in a state of near ecstasy. At last, there was a focus in my life that concurred with all the doctrines I had been taught! My feet trailed lightly up a little side street, toward the centre of the town and, from there, the carriage home. With downcast eyes, the narrow, cobbled street seemed as if it were mile upon mile below me. A terrible teratism had finally lost its grip on me. Steps angelic; heavenly. A liquid sun wept and bled; in the east cherubim and seraphim guarded a tree bearing strange fruit. Between us, a flaming sword turning, as I turned. Diaphanous mists, as delicate as lace; clouds. A holy tree, beckoning. Streams of fire emanating from the rubied enclaves of Endymion, cloaking the land in flames of elemental purgation. Burning, in the robe of Nessus, burning! A strange calling. Onwards; upwards; reptiles groaning. Cherubs falling like rain. Centuries of dust and sand, congealed and conspiratorial. Half-glimpsed shapes. Funeral pyres burning my corpse on branches torn from the Tree of Life.

When I opened my eyes, a dark and indistinct figure stood over me, yet a shape familiar, a shape I thought had cast me aside: Sebastian.

Temptation

Looking around, I sought to make sense of it all. The tree, the sword, the fruit, and the cherub were all gone. I lay where I had fallen: at the side of the road. It took no more than a few brief moments to register that it had all been a waking dream. Finally, Sebastian pierced the silence.

"Well, it has been a long time."

"Sebastian, you look dreadful," I said, causing him to laugh.

"Well, thank you." His once handsome visage had become gaunt and drawn. His clothes clung to him like tattered rags on a corpse. His fingernails were long, broken, and so filthy one might have suspected he had been tilling soil. Even his eyes were dull. "I am ashes where once I was fire." He affected a theatrical pose before his lips parted and, once again, a smile spread across his face. It was wonderful to see him. It felt as though a fresh breeze had blown away the autumn leaves of uncertainty.

"What have you been doing?" he asked. As he spoke, I realised I was still lying in the gutter by the side of the road. It seemed ironic that I should be contemplating his fall from grace when mine appeared to have laid me equally low. I wanted to tell him that I was about to enter the church but felt acutely embarrassed at having to say so, or that I had even considered it.

"What have *you* been doing?" It was the best

answer I could think of as I sensed his question had been rhetorical. He didn't answer but, instead, extended a hand and helped me to my feet.

"I know," he said casually.

"Know what?" I knew what he meant, my face burning with embarrassment.

"What your plans are." It was unnerving and seemed as though every thought I thought had been written down for him to read.

"My … my ..." I began to stammer. My stammer would betray me if nothing else would.

"Come on, don't stammer! I'm not your father. You've no need to be frightened of my response. Just don't think you can keep it from me. I know you plan to join the church." I didn't know how he knew, only that he did. What could I say? To tell him he was mistaken would have been a lie; to tell him that I was, would have been to betray myself as weak and someone in need of such a crutch. "I'm not going to condemn you for it. You must follow the path that is right for *you*. If you think that what you're doing is right, go ahead - with my blessing. That said, you and I both know that it is not really what you want. You want freedom. Are you going to get that by entering a prison?"

"But I can *never* be free - not now. Too much has happened. I can't make a single decision without thinking 'what would so and so want me to do', or 'is this right as a Christian'? I've had so many absolutes foisted upon me I've lost my identity. Everything would be so much easier if I surrendered completely."

"Nobody said it would be easy. Without God, life is anguish, abandonment, and despair but that is the price we pay if we want freedom. Life is oh so cosy, isn't it, when you have universal laws of right and wrong to guide you on your way? Well, let me tell you, nothing is *ever* as straightforward as that. Even murder might be right in the right circumstances. For me, the great object of life is sensation - to feel we exist, even if in pain." By now he had straightened up and had begun walking, taking me with him. With his gaze set on the ground in front of him, every word seemed deliberate and well-chosen, as though he were wrestling with each one so that he could clarify his point as clearly as possible, lest any ambiguities elicited a confused understanding on my part.

As he spoke, his words sliced me like a sabre. On an instinctive level, they seemed true yet all I had been taught considered them wrong. Dual feelings began tearing me apart. I knew my failings, but the brutal way Sebastian had confronted them was crushing. I hated myself for being weak and hypocritical. I hated my father for forging me into something I despised. I was a mess; a wreck, incapable of taking control of the forces within my own life. I had been tyrannised, bullied, beaten; my will crushed to annihilation. Every action I had ever made had been prey to scorn, derision and mockery by him or, conversely, unwarranted praise by those who could see the effect his actions had on me. All I ever wanted was the truth! How could Sebastian advocate self-creation without acknowledging *those* factors?

Tears began to roll down my face. Not tears of physical pain, but tears of loss, hopelessness, frustration, and rage. I had lost something apparently irretrievable. I clung to my refuge, and he to me.

"I really think we need to talk about a few things, but you've got to believe in me," he continued.

"I do, I do." Nervously, I laughed. Sebastian straightened. Almost at once, he seemed reanimated and colour flushed his cheeks. I knew I needed something beyond time, space, and reality: something deep and arcane. At the bottom of my soul burned fires of rage, indignation, and torment; of something hopelessly crestfallen yet still proud and noble. If he could nurture all that I wasn't going to turn him away.

"Then meet me in your garden tonight." My thoughts seemed to drift away into the cool evening, thoughts as heady and intoxicating as the finest opium. Destiny began to unfold itself like a giant magic carpet. In what seemed like an instant, Sebastian was gone.

My ride home was swift, my mind too alive to notice my surroundings or the passing of time; I was travelling on a journey of greater magnitude. Finally, I turned the road that approached my house but as soon

Temptation

as I saw it standing dark and resolute against the mountain and dark trees my heart seemed to leap into my throat, and all the fears of childhood came surging back. Clattering across the night sky, hooves from ghostly, unseen nags. Desperate, baying, howling hounds. High above, in the evening empyrean, sunbeams flowed like tears. Who will mourn the death of the white hart and a loss of innocence? Now, to return to satisfied smiles that celebrated unreal kingdoms.

How I made it from the carriage I shall never know, nor how I made it to the house and opened the door that penetrated the inner sanctum. A huge and hellish fire glowed and spat in the hearth like molten iron. No other light, other than the one in the grate, lit the room leaving much of the room in an awful gloom, neither light nor dark. Reality; unreality. Flames hungrily consumed the once-living wood so that it hissed and cracked in apparent agony. Then, the figure that ruled this ghastly place.

"I'm ... I'm ... I'm home." Once I had struggled to get the words out, they left a taste in my mouth as bitter as wormwood. Home? This was no home! I knew that to say anything untoward would only bring his awful twisted wrath down upon me.

"Stop stammering. What are you? A man, or a nervous girl?" His reply was nasal and droning. He moved, seemingly tearing his head away from the winged armchair that had previously kept it from my view. With a slowness terrible to look upon, that head turned until the eyes upon its face met with mine. Sickeningly pallid cheeks seemed to reflect the flames of the fire to such a degree that his whole appearance seemed scalded.

"Where's my mother?" The question fell upon ears that refused to listen.

"You needn't think you're going to spend the whole time under my feet. I've made arrangements for you to attend Bible classes. You might think yourself a man, but you're *nothing*. Maybe the scriptures will make something of you, for I cannot."

With that, he slumped back into the chair. The chief prosecutor had spoken: my fate appeared sealed.

"Where is my mother?" My temerity unnerved me. He still refused to answer. "What has happened to her?"

"Shut your damned mouth! As the great St. Paul said, 'Let the woman learn in silence with all subjection. But I suffer not a woman to teach, nor to usurp the authority of a man, but to be in silence. For Adam was first formed, then Eve. And Adam was not deceived, but the woman being deceived was in the transgression'. She transgressed if you must know. That woman was as worthless as you. I refuse to believe you're *my* offspring." He leaned forward, like some rabid canine. "Why should I - a pious man - have to suffer iniquities in my house? Get out of my sight! You're an offence to me and the Lord."

If I had any doubts about the way I felt, by now they had been fully dispelled. I turned silently away and walked to the garden. Down the steps, a turn right, past the lawn. At first, the stillness of the night made everything appear tranquil. Then, from the shadows, a figure that had been stood by the gate stepped into the last rays of a dying, crepuscular, sun. The great iron edifice swung open and free behind him.

"You wanted to speak to me?" I began before emotion threatened to choke me. Like he who wishes to put an end to life's pale vicissitudes, I felt both anguish and yet a strange calm knowing the race was almost done, like a man holding a loaded gun: unable to go on, yet comforted in knowing that in his hand he has the means to draw a final line under his existence.

Sebastian extended an arm and bade me welcome, gesturing that we both should go beyond the boundary marked by the edge of the lawn and the steps beyond. I wanted him to speak: to allay my fears. I had always known this temptation would be one to which one day I would succumb. Whatever happened now, it did not matter as *nothing* mattered anymore.

I took a step, then paused. What would happen next? If I were to reject my whole education then what would replace it? In doing so, might I lose *myself*? Already, it felt too late to go back. I took a deep breath and closed my eyes, allowing Sebastian to take my arm and guide me. I don't know what I expected but after a few brief moments, mustered the courage to open my eyes only to find myself deep in a darkening forest. Initially, it felt as though I were alone as I had lost all trace of the narrow path. Shadows that I had once feared, as silent as the grave, seemed to envelop me in verdant arms like a mother nurturing an infant.

"Sebastian!" In the darkness I could see his indistinct outline, drawing nearer, becoming more definite. He didn't answer: perhaps that was the way of one grown feeble from long being mute.

"We need to make our own path if we want to be clear of this place," he said, taking my arm and leading me toward the copse from whence he had stepped. The velvet canopy above us was so dense it appeared to be a thick brocade stretching upward and around us like a soft blanket. Somewhere, high above us, branches moved like swaying limbs allowing near-pellucid silver shafts to light our way. Here we were safe in this unspoilt cocoon. From liquid night, from darkest shade, Sebastian again stepped toward me.

"Let's sit down. I want to talk to you about your faith." He made his way to a clearing and sat, making himself comfortable, before he continued.

"How do you think religion began?" The question seemed a rhetorical one as before I could answer he continued. "Let us go back to the origins of all religions. We understand now, that people die from all manner of unseen causes, but did people always think like that? What of the person who sees her, apparently healthy, offspring perish for, ostensibly, no reason and an old man survive? What conclusion would the savage mind have come to, seeing seemingly healthy young people die, and sick, elderly, people recover? Of course, knowing little of medicine, the reasons were not explicable by natural causes, but by the supernatural. Thus, evil or good forces were deemed to have willed events to have occurred. Disease, attack, a good or bad harvest, were nothing more than the agents by which those malignant or benevolent forces manifested themselves." He paused for breath and nodded to me for me to acknowledge my understanding. I nodded back. "Now, far from God making man in his own image - which is a ludicrous vanity of man - humanity - typically - made gods in *their* image. Initially, gods were the souls of trees, plants, and animals, all of whom were propitiated as they ensured the primitive's life or death. How long before the tree-spirit became a forest-god? This is an important change, for, after losing its tenancy over any one particular tree, the forest-god became an abstract figure. I'm sure you'd agree with me that humanity's one proclivity is to clothe abstract forms with concrete human shapes."

"Go on. I think I follow you." It didn't seem as profound as what Sebastian had to say, but I was anxious for him to continue. He smiled and brought his hand to his mouth, as though he were struggling with his thoughts before continuing.

"Already then, we have nature gods. How long do you think it would have been before those gods were venerated? How long before every good or bad spirit was subordinated to a good or bad god?" He paused again, before standing.

"Sebastian?" It appeared as though he were about to walk away. He raised a finger to his pursed lips, gesturing for my silence.

"So then, the early gods associated with plants and animals, by their nature, must have been associated with the continued survival of whichever plant or animal with which they were associated. Continued survival necessitated procreativity and fertility. Thus, many of the early gods were fertility gods, because they ensured survival in what were often very hard circumstances. Nearer our own time, Plato posited a theory of 'Ideal Forms'. Loosely, his idea was that heaven - though not the conditional Christian Heaven - had the perfect image of everything we have on earth. We, in the world of matter, had only pale shadows of these originals. Thus, in Platonic thought, matter was deemed inferior to spirit. Couple this idea with the earthly, carnal gods of fertility, and how long do you think it would be before those gods came to be vilified? Look at Pan - half-man, half-goat, with hairy legs, horns, cloven hooves, huge genitals! Now, where have I seen *that* image before?" His face affected confusion before breaking into a smile. "I tell you, the god of the old religion always becomes the devil of the new. Look at what the Christians of the middle-ages did to those warm, sensual gods of nature - they turned them into demons. Do you know why fertility cults were suppressed? Because the faith of Judaism, virtually appropriated by Christianity, considered immortality as attainable only through one's offspring. As they say, 'It's a wise father that knows his own child'. That's why that faith esteemed a faithful woman 'far above rubies'. Do you think fertility cults would have been so suppressed if it were men who bore the child? Of course not! They would have been sure their offspring were theirs, so faithfulness and the absurd notion that the only virtuous woman is *virgo intacta* would not have even been a cause of concern."

"God forbid!"

"Yes, unfortunately, he does!" We laughed, as I leaned back on my elbows, and stretched out my legs. Again, I wanted to let him continue, lest I break his flow of thought.

"Look at the Devil and God." By now, he was becoming more animated. Pacing up and down, he began to use his hands to reinforce the spoken word. "Both of them evolved from nature Gods, with a little help from Persia and the Old Testament. In the early years of Christianity, many people thought of God and the Devil as equal powers, given that good cannot create evil. This was eventually deemed heretical since no power could be equal to God. In the year five-sixty-three, the Council of Braga decided that no power could be equal to God since God created *everything*. If that is the case, then God *must* have created evil! Some versions of the Bible have God saying, in Isiah forty-five and seven, 'I form the light and create darkness. I make peace and create evil. I, the Lord, do all these things'. We might well ask ourselves what sort of a monster God really is, given that little outburst! On the other hand, many Biblical passages also acknowledge God's failure to administer power on earth. Doesn't John twelve and thirty-one, call Satan 'Prince of this world?' Corinthians four and four, goes even further, calling Satan 'God of this world'. Not bad for a former nature spirit!" Sebastian's face creased into a smile. He paused and looked to the ground. "Can you see where this is leading?" He seemed concerned that he should speak with clarity.

"Yes, of course." It seemed obvious that he was stripping away the sacred aspect of Christianity, explaining it as nothing more than one of many creation myths.

"In Matthew four and nine, we find Satan taking Christ to the top of a mountain to show him the world, promising 'All these things I will give thee if thou wilt fall down and worship me' and it is quite explicit that such treasures are Satan's to give but - really - what nonsense! And it is this passage - along with a few others - that led to the *supposed* worship of Satan and the *actual* torture, rape, murder and cruelty inflicted on thousands of innocent people by Christians during the Witch-Hunts and Inquisition. Let's look at the Bible: have you noticed just how many inconsistencies there are within those pages? Let's stay with the Devil. Doesn't Matthew thirteen and forty-two, call hell 'a furnace of fire' whilst Job ten and twenty-one calls it 'a land of darkness, of darkness itself'. Not a great inconsistency, perhaps, but there *are* some important ones.

"The Biblical account of creation says God made the world in five days, then on the sixth day made man, before resting on the seventh. Isn't this flatly contradicted in Genesis, chapter two, which tells us that God made heaven and earth, then he made Man? On the third day came the Garden of Eden, fourthly came the beasts and fowl and lastly the forming of a woman from a man's rib. This second version gave us Eve, supposedly responsible for The Fall. Perhaps that is why Anselm of Canterbury wrote 'woman has a lovely face and a lovely form. She pleases you not a little this milk-white creature! But ah! If her bowels were opened and all the regions of her flesh, what foul tissues would this white skin be shown to contain'. Needless to say, Anselm is held in high esteem by the church! You think the Bible an upholder of virtue? Then ask yourself who

Adam and Eve's sons married. Having children with one's own sister - a sister not even worthy of being named! - was obviously not as great a sin as stealing a loaf of bread to feed one's starving family, or worshipping a god of one's own choosing.

"Because of the absurd notion that, in the guise of the serpent, and as 'God of this world', Satan bad the ability to offer secret knowledge, the scientific quest was - for centuries - thought to be acquired only with the Devil's help. This condemned many to lives of disease, poverty, desperation, and ignorance. St. Paul - as we might expect - even denied women pain relief in childbirth, thinking that, given Eve's `transgression' woman shall be saved in child-bearing thanks to a passage in Genesis that states 'in sorrow thou shalt bring forth children'. Now, let us look at this matter. If, for a moment, we put aside the knowledge that Christianity only developed from paganism and that God is the divine creator then what can we say of God? Given all the atrocities in the world, we must conclude that God either *wills* such events or is *powerless* to do anything to prevent them. Given the latter is impossible - because a Christian God is seen as omnipotent - we must conclude that God *wills* these atrocities. I know that you may say 'God gave us free will so it is us who are at fault', but what sort of a monster would not stay the hand of a cold-blooded murderer if it were in his power to do so?

"I'm sure you're well aware of the 'Thou shalt

not suffer a witch to live', in Exodus twenty-two and eighteen. Intolerant, you might say, but what would you say upon realising that in Paulian Christianity *anyone* not of Paulian faith was deemed a witch? At various times Jews, Muslims, Cathars, Waldenses, Albigenses, Manicheists have all been called witches. Protestants and Catholics have even called each other by the name! Would St. Paul have had them all killed? And what of pagan witches? No witch worships the Christian Devil! The Devil is a part of the Christian tradition so why would a pagan witch - often knowing *nothing* of Christianity - worship a Christian Devil? Do you know why the Witch Hunts and the Inquisition were so popular? Because it gave those in a position of power a rod with which to break the backs of the poor people that they deemed undesirable. Religion had *nothing* to do with it even if that was the name under which it was perpetrated - it was simply persecution. As we might have expected from such a misogynistic creed, many of the victims were women, but what did that matter? It wasn't until the Council of Trent met in the middle of the sixteenth century, that women were even deemed to have souls! Even then, it was only passed by a majority of three!" Sebastian let out a sigh, and sat down, next to my recumbent form.

"I find that unbelievable," I said after waiting a while to see if he'd finished. There had been so many facts in what he had said and every one seemed more extreme than the last. Just what sort of a faith had twisted my lifelong thinking?

"I know. If you read it in a novel you might disbelieve it, but every word is true. How can we have any respect for people who carry on that tradition?" He looked at me with raised eyebrows and an inquisitive look. I knew to whom he was alluding.

"Well, even the Devil can quote scripture for his own ends", I muttered, pondering what he had said.

"Yes, I can. I mean, yes, *he* can", Sebastian said, accentuating what he had said with an inscrutable wink.

"Have you finished?" I wished to avert his attention.

"No. Look what God has done to the Devil - the fallen angel who dared to question the authority of God, and who was then cast into the pit, to forever rail against a smugly triumphant power. Is that a God of forgiveness and mercy? It's not even a god of law and justice. It's the act of a monster.

"But do you know what? I hate the fact that Christianity capitalises on people's fear of death by promising conditional immortality. It's only a form of control perpetuated by those in power. Be a good boy and you'll go to heaven but be a bad boy and you'll go to hell. It's the greatest confidence trick ever!"

With that, we both fell silent. For a long time, both of us stared at the floor in quiet contemplation. Finally. Sebastian spoke.

Temptation

"Come on. Let's head home." He stood up and offered a hand to help me to my feet. This time, however, I was able to rise unaided. Sebastian smiled.

As we entered again the sweet, summer garden, things appeared to have altered: again, the garden provided the solace I had felt as a child. Suddenly, a door slammed causing Sebastian to pull me into the shadows.

"It's your father," he said, his eyes training upon the sinister figure at the top of the steps, a figure scouring the garden. Sebastian raised a finger to his lips, gesturing for my silence.

"What's he doing?" My whisper was hoarse.

"If you be quiet for a moment, we'll see."

Satisfied that the garden was empty, the threatening shape that towered above us locked the back door and made his way to the road upon which, just a few hours before, I had walked.

"I'm going to follow him. Come on." I said, but Sebastian stood firm. "What? What is it?" If we were to follow, we needed to take our leave quickly,

"I think you should go alone. You don't need me."

"Why do you say that?" Already I knew there would be no convincing him otherwise. "Are you going to come with me, or not?"

"No." He bowed his head. "You go. I'll meet you here tomorrow."

Temptation

There was no time to argue. If I delayed my leaving any longer the hope of a pursuit would be lost.

I ascended the steps, quickly, and silently made my way to the road. There, in the distance, was the dark silhouette I wished to follow. It wasn't long before my nocturnal pursuit took on a more concerted, obvious, purpose. No longer did the figure in front of me appear to be out for a midnight saunter. There was reason and purpose in his manner and - judging by the numerous furtive glances - a very secret purpose to his journey.

A mist that had covered the whole area was beginning to lift. As we entered the old part of the town that led down to the river, there was a final glance over his shoulder before the shape in front made an abrupt turn up a squalid side street. I had to keep up with him and tried to silently run on the old cobblestones. Despite the mist, I could see quite clearly. Suddenly, he stopped and looked behind in what, I thought, was my direction. I hid in the shadows. Quickly, he removed a key from a pocket before leaning close to a door and trying to open it. I was close enough to hear the key fall to the ground. In the moonlight, it shone, like a fish in a dark pool. Stooping, he picked up his lost trophy. This time, however, the door opened for him. Like Jonah and the whale, he was quickly swallowed and the door closed behind him, I made my way to the window of the house my father had entered. Three figures sat at a table, in the middle of the sparsely furnished room. Moving to give myself a better vantage point, one face came into view: Lillian! The object of my unrequited love sat opposite two figures, both of whom had their backs to me.

"Lillian, go to your room," a woman barked before standing and gesturing toward the stairs. No sooner had the young woman left, then the figure I had followed through the darkened streets thrust himself upon his female companion, frantically tearing at her clothes, whilst she - laughing - eased open her fastenings, hastening the work of his clumsy fingers. Pulling the woman to the floor, both sets of hands then set to unbuttoning his attire. Lank hair fell upon bleached and pitted skin. I had seen enough; I turned and made my way home.

Next day was spent in my garden; it was as it had been when I was a child. I was desperately worried about my mother and where she might be as she'd still not returned home. I'd made up my mind that if she had not returned by the following day, I would visit her acquaintances and see if she was with them but a dreadful, empty feeling told me something awful might have happened. Ought I to have acted on that hunch so soon? It was difficult to know. With the lengthening shades of the afternoon, an indistinct contour appeared on the road, before stepping nearer: it was my friend, Sebastian.

"I'm not sure about this," he said, despite his

voice betraying no sense of uncertainty.

"About what?" I didn't remember asking him to do anything for me.

"About going to that house with you tonight."

"How do you know about that house? How did you know I even *intended* going there again, and that I was going to ask you to come with me?" It unnerved me. How did he know?

"Am I wrong, then?" Always, he seemed so assured.

"Well, you know you don't have to come if you don't want to, but why don't you?"

"I feel as though I'm intruding. There's a bond of blood that I can never be a part of. You should go and go *alone*," his final word seeming to echo all around me.

"Well, I *am* going. Will you stay here?"

"Of course - *always*." Again, his final word had a resonance.

I stepped out of the familiar confines and was soon making my way through the darkening streets, the silence as harrowing as a distant howl. It was a clear night: a full moon, in fact. Although the road I had to take I had seldom walked before it seemed known to me. It lay before me, like a shining river making its way to the ocean. Sebastian's sombre mood had sapped my enthusiasm, leaving me enervated. Like a cat stalking a bird, though, enthusiasm played no part in the actions - it was instinctive.

Temptation

Soon I came to the Norman gate that separated the outlying areas from the town. Clouds, like sepia-tinged funereal veils, that previously shrouded the moon were gone: my way was illuminated.

Something deep and primitive had become a welcome guest somewhere within me. For the first time, it felt as though there was something *whole* taking charge and shaping my destiny – and that thing was me. At last, I had recognised my gaoler, executioner, and undertaker. Freedom would finally come only upon the destruction of that unholy trinity.

There was the little house. I knew who would be there. In the still of the night, one light burned, high above me, the rest of the house lying as dark as a spent seam in one of the local coal mines. I clambered up, and then upon, a porch that happened to be fortuitously placed beneath the window from which the light emerged. From there I could see everything.

There, standing proud above a tiny single bed, was my father. Beneath him, blankets barely covered a form, yet not covering the face I instantly recognised as Lillian's. A sickening, familiar smile flushed his bloated face as he began to undo his belt. One brief sentence unfolded the entire story. Cowering under the thin fabric, one pitiful strain broke the night air.

"No, Dad, no."

That one utterance transformed our lives. The girl for whom I had harboured a passion was a product of the same loins as me. I had loved my sister! Now her father - our father - was about to ... no, it was too horrible to contemplate. He had bullied, tyrannised, and dominated everyone, in whatever way he could. His hands, his religion, his masculinity, were all tools to be used to gratify his own ends.

What was to be done? Could I just stand by, like God, when it was within my power to stop it? How could any god allow *this* to happen and stand idly aside? It sickened me. If I stood by and did nothing then that would make me as bad as that god. If need be, I had to die stopping him.

Punching a hole in the glass, the next thing I remember was facing the man. The initial shatter had caused him some little surprise and he had clutched his waistcoat around himself. His countenance soon changed to a sneer as I made a grab for him - and missed. Everything I hated, everything I could possibly hate, lay housed in that hideous frame in front of me. That face; that sneer.

"Leave her alone ... you destroyed my mother, you destroyed me. You're not going to destroy her as well." Rage made my face throb; my eyes pulsed with the racing rhythm of my pounding heart; the collar of my shirt pressing hard against the bulging veins in my neck.

"Well! Not stuttering for once, girl? Wha ... wha ... wha ... what's it got to do with you? You're both daughters of mine and I'll do what the hell I like with you both." The mocking in his voice broke into a laugh.

Those words - that admission - sealed his fate. I knew then I would either kill or be killed.

"Now, get out!" The smirk on his face withered to a bloody wrath before he laughed again - laughed at my powerlessness; laughed at his oppression. Frozen, I remained motionless. Anger shattered that laugh.

He stepped forward and with a huge, hammering blow, struck me across the side of the head. Everything else in the room faded into darkness. Now, there was just the two of us. The force of the knock had sent me reeling into a wall. Before I could recover, his huge red face came bearing down on me, his wide mouth roaring and slavering.

"Come on, what are you going to do?" I remembered how he had pulled me to the ground and bellowed in my face when I was a child when I had bought him a birthday gift and had tried to sneak that gift into the house without his knowing. He had demanded to know and I, not wishing to spoil the surprise, wouldn't tell. That had been the last gift he had ever received from me. Now, the impotent rage I had long suppressed welled-up inside me and I threw him off and leapt to my feet. Unarmed, I would be killed.

I looked for something; anything. The walls? There! There hung a huge, heavy crucifix. I ran toward it, clutched it from its fixings, turned, and with a heavy swing, powered by all the force I could muster, brought it down upon the side of his head. The wound opened up like a stigmata. Trickling at first, then spurting like a crimson stream onto his open shirt.

He stumbled backwards, placing his coarse fingers to the hole, without uttering a sound. He fell to the side of the bed, his blood staining the thin cotton sheets. His discarded apparel fell from the bed and into his life's flow. I looked at Lillian. We stared at each other in mute horror. She looked away as the figure slumped on the floor. I followed her gaze. Somehow, from somewhere, the man had found new life. Before he had the opportunity of a reprise, I ran forward. With all the strength I could muster that old rugged cross was brought down again and again. Every strike opened his wound a little wider, every crisp retort opening the door of the cage that had always locked away the real me. Firm skin and bone gave way to splintered wood and torn blanket, both saturated in blood. Then a bang; a flash of flame; a warm wetness spreading itself across my chest.

In my enthusiasm, I had not noticed the little pistol in his hand. Somehow, in those final moments, nerves - or the contractions of his muscles in their death agony - had managed to squeeze the trigger. The cross dropped from my hand; the hole in my chest began to weep. I looked at he who had fired: hideously the shape, having stood, now began to slide down the wall sideways, before the whole figure hinged at the hip as it negotiated the open space of the broken window. Already dead, the figure sat motionless for a moment. Finally, gravity alone pulled the figure backwards. Like the drop of a sack of grain, a dull thud told us it had hit the pavement below.

So, we come to the present. The last few days have been odd. Sometimes I am aware that I lie in a hospital bed, guards at the door. Other times it feels as though I am home, in my garden: in the eternal Summerland of childhood - or at least those first few years of freedom.

Sebastian? Has Sebastian ever really existed outside of my own imagination? He was the natural and unrecognised aspect of my personality made flesh and blood. Only now that I feel whole can I acknowledge that he was the ideal construct of my mind and all that I wished to be. As the philosopher said, 'Art is long and life is short'. If that is true then Sebastian will live forever for all that can ever survive of us is our imagination and the things that precious gift leaves behind. In this insane, Godless, world he had been the voice of sanity.

Lillian, I am told, has been to visit me but some sort of criminal collusion is suspected so her visits have been denied. What sick mind found gratification in throwing the two of us together in that awful, twisted school?

Now, however, I must stop as I am growing so

very weak. Free at last - yet dying. How ironic! The two appear uncomfortable companions for an atheist, yet both are singing, melodiously, sweetly. Mother is beckoning. I must follow. Free - finally free.

Denial

Denial

What is the worst of woes that wait on age?
What stamps the wrinkle deeper on the brow?
To view each loved one blotted from life's page,
And be alone on earth as I am now.

Byron

Denial

In the old house, high on the Welsh mountain, Lillian sat at a large, carved, and age-darkened desk. Dipping a fountain pen in a small pot of ink she began to write in a beautifully cursive hand, softly speaking the words as she wrote: "I am a sick woman. I am an evil woman. Thorns of melancholy pierce my heart. All I have is the fragile permanence of a few last and precious words. Love has survived he who wrote them, as it survives us all. I remain - unnatural, hateful, insane. No part of nature flows within me."

Lillian closed the journal she had only recently begun to keep and walked from her desk to a window at the far end of the room. From there she could see the whole panorama of the garden, the garden where once her brother had walked. She was still unsure of the house. Until recently it had been peopled by her father and his family, a family of whom she had known nothing. Death had given her wealth. Her father had not intended a woman get his property, but a catalogue of misfortune - his death, the death of his son, a mysterious disappearance - had all left Lillian the sole beneficiary. She had once dreamt of escape: to leave her awful little house behind and live in luxury. Yet luxury was a bloodless consort: she would have traded it all for a life of even moderate happiness. Inside her, there was nothing: a void; a well of loneliness. A feeling familiar to those who yearn to love.

It was raining. Now, the pane of glass that

separated her from the outside world had become opaque. Outside, the world remained as cloudy as her warm breath as it hit the cold glass, only to confuse her view of the world even more. Without realising, she raised a finger to etch idly upon her pane. How might life have been if only she had been different; if circumstances had been different? She felt small, frail, vulnerable and alone. It seemed as if some imminent catastrophe, worse than death, awaited her. Suddenly, her eyes focussed on her aimless finger's ramblings: why on earth had she written 'Sebastian'?

"Sebastian," she mouthed silently, her lips barely moving. Her brother's journal had come into her possession and she had read it; she knew the name from that. "Sebastian." What could Sebastian be to her? Perhaps it was that all the other figures in her brother's journal were unfleshed skeletons compared with his depiction, or maybe it was because he alone remained. Who was he? Had he *really* been nothing more than a figment of her brother's imagination? If he was real, would he one day pay her a visit? So much remained uncertain. In her rational moments she told herself that he did not exist yet her heart hoped he did - with a passion - and when has passion ever been a slave to rationality? Deep within her, she wanted him to be real: for him to come to her and make everything right.

Shadows that only the dying rays of an early evening sun can bring had already entered the room. In the eerie gloom, dark shapes were becoming threatening; dangerous. Images seen from the corner of an eye had a life. Only when her attention focussed on them did they lose their terror. Lillian closed her eyes but that was worse as shapes then took on the form of hideous caricatures of her father. She lit a lamp. She could never run away from what had happened because it was a part of her. If only she had never been born, then both her father and brother might still be alive. Sometimes, she sought to shift the burden of guilt to another's shoulders but there was still a bond of blood which, even if she could hate the perpetrator, resulted in her hating herself because a part of him walked with her. The little flame, however, was bright enough to expel the night terrors. Now the room took on a gentle glow. With a swift motion, Lillian turned and drew the curtains. Now she felt safe: shut away from the world.

She had lived alone in the old house now for a few months. It had taken almost a year for her father's finances to be put in order but now that they finally had she found herself a considerably wealthy young woman. Nonetheless, the wealth had become a curse that seemed to have a strange and terrible obligation binding her to it.

Night, with all its dark dominions, is never an easy time especially when every night is a fraught and restless one. As her brother had noted in his journal, the old house groaned and creaked more than most. Now, however, its terrible history populated it with many an unhappy revenant. Sometimes it felt as though she were being buried alive, the cold damp soil failing relentlessly upon the casket in which she felt immured, she being the only living thing amongst century upon century of the dead. Already, the house had begun to drain any enthusiasm she had once had for life. Days became agonies only to be endured. Every night the same pestilence descended upon her lonely rooms.

Another restless night found Lillian arise unusually early. A slight chink in the curtains had allowed the first unruly rays of the sun to tenderly touch the white blankets of her bed. Falling upon her face, those same rays slowly melted the frozen wasteland, thawing despair.

Her bedroom had been one of the rooms little used, prior to the property becoming hers. It had once been a guest room but as the previous occupants had shunned guests the room had lain dormant for many years. It was the only room she felt had not been violated. It was a room on which she could stamp her identity rather than feeling crushed by the weight of another's. She liked its asexuality. So many other rooms in the house had become gendered, suggesting male oppression and female subjugation. If the room appeared sexless, however, Lillian did not. Despite all she had been through, her appearance gave no indication of the troubled waters beneath the calm surface, a calm surface that radiated a sensuality.

Something small and almost intangible had, with the sun's rays, shifted the pivot of her world. Her equilibrium - the indefinable scales of the mind that shifted from despair to elation in an instant - had balanced. For the first time in years, she began to feel positive.

The sun had awoken a multitude of slumbering creatures. Now, the whole room seemed teeming with new life. Through one tiny gap, Lillian could see that the new day had performed the same miracle in her garden. It was still very early, so dew still hung like tiny tears upon every green leaf and stem. Now, a loving hand had begun to wipe them away.

Lillian pulled back the sheets and bounded downstairs and raced toward the door. In the garden, the dew of the new day's grass made her giddy; unsteady upon her bare feet, like a newborn deer and like a deer, every ungainly step seemed a joyous celebration.

Dancing; whirling. Something *had* changed, something of which Lillian was not even aware. All the while that change watched from the dawn shadows: Sebastian had returned.

Laughing, and with feet wet from the damp grass, Lillian fell to the ground running her fingers through each strand as one might run one's fingers through the hair of a lover, every sensuous touch more exhilarating than the last. It was then her gaze met the eyes of he who had been watching her.

The laughter stopped. She had wanted to scream but could only lie still and transfixed. The gloriously black pupils of her eyes widened and her soft lips parted, yet remained silent. All the while, Sebastian did nothing save return her gaze. Shadows played upon his form as a gentle breeze caused the tree he stood beneath to quiver. Protean, it appeared that just for a moment as if *he* were also changing. Finally, Lillian spoke.

"Sebastian?" There was no answer. The young man continued to gaze upon the supine woman in front of him. Her voice had registered like a heavy blow: like the voice of his own soul.

"Are you Sebastian?" Lillian said the words with slow deliberation, as though she were talking to someone who she feared could not understand her. The silence made her uneasy. Something else unsettled her: for a long time, it had felt as though stagnant water had coursed her veins. Now? Now it felt as if a new life spring flowed through them, washing away every impurity.

"Yes." The reply was clear and distinct, and with a resonance that could move worlds. The brevity of the reply did nothing to allay the feeling of anxious anticipation Lillian felt as she brought herself to a sitting position. Here was a man she felt to be, at least partially, responsible for the death of her brother yet she could not help feeling fatally attracted to him. Maybe he could answer her questions, once she had the courage to ask them.

Sebastian stepped from the cool shadows. Lillian, instinctively, moved away. He had brought about a collapse into ruins of so many people. She felt drawn to him, yet wished him to banish him. He reminded her of things she laboured to forget.

The bright sunshine washed over the lithe young man swathing his features in light. He was everything her brother had described, yet somehow different. Lillian found it difficult to determine yet there was something, she felt, that her brother had missed.

"And you?" Lillian had quite forgotten that in asking his name she had not given her own.

"Lillian." Her voice trembled slightly. She felt the statement needed to be qualified as though her name, her identity, were not enough. "I live here. This is my house."

"Where is ...?"

"Dead." Lillian anticipated the question.

"Dead?" Sebastian staggered, temporarily losing his balance, before reaching out a hand to a tree to steady himself. Lillian flushed hot and cold. The way she had broken the news had been insensitive. She had assumed Sebastian would have known or, at least, guessed. She remembered how she had felt when she had first heard. Now, her heart went out to him.

"I'm sorry. Didn't you know?" Her voice indicated concern but remained aloof. After all, however well she thought she knew Sebastian, in actuality, he was a stranger.

"No. No. You must be mistaken." Sebastian's voice was not yet desperate. His reply indicated disbelief, but of the kind one intones when given any fact one believes to be false.

Lilian shook her head, letting her gaze fall to her feet.

"Where is he? He's got to be alive." The rise in pitch told Lillian that, regardless of what Sebastian said, he now knew her words to be true.

"No." Her soft voice shallow.

"Tell me." Sebastian took a step toward Lillian. She, feeling threatened, retreated. Sebastian's tone was becoming desperate and accusing.

"It's your fault. You left him when he needed you most." The moment Lillian uttered the words, she regretted every syllable. It was wrong of her to apportion blame. Now the words made her mouth sting. If they did that to her, what had they done to him? She looked for a reaction upon his face, but there was none. Sebastian turned and strode toward the gate, the same gate that had figured so prominently in her brother's journal.

"Wait ..." Lillian wanted to run after him but her pride would not let her do so. Before she could say another word, Sebastian spun around, interrupting her.

"So, it's *my* fault, is it? Am I my brother's keeper?" Sebastian's emotions were running high. Now, his tone became hostile.

"No, you're not." It wasn't an apology but the nearest she could come to one.

"Thank you." The tone of the words was

sarcastic, yet with them, his whole body appeared to relax. There had been a moment of shock when she had first told him of the death but that had now been replaced by an uneasy calm. The sun caught his green eyes as they scrutinised the young woman in front of him.

"I know your name is Sebastian, but who *are* you?" The question needed to be asked, for, despite all she knew, Sebastian remained an enigma.

"Sebastian." A wry smile followed. If Lillian had expected the question to reveal the inner workings of a soul, she now realised those workings would not be revealed with one simple question.

"Yes. I know your name is Sebastian, but who are you?" Perhaps if she persisted a little more may be revealed. The smile dropped from his face and, once again, he turned away. Lillian thought to ask again would be unwise and was about to desist when, unexpectedly, a reply came.

"I can't say." The words seemed pitiful and tragic. It didn't appear that Sebastian was unwilling to say but that he could not say because he really did not know.

"You don't know?" Her voice was gentle and coaxing.

"No, but aren't we all such stuff as dreams are made of?" It didn't tell Lillian a lot, if anything,

"Are you trying to tell me you're a dream?"

"No, more a creation of the mind."

"How can a mind create ...?" Once again, her sentence was preempted.

"Doesn't a mind create *everything*? How can anything be perceived other than through the mind? It is only the senses that make anything real." Sebastian spoke the words with conviction, as though he had given the subject his every thought for a long time. Lillian paused to consider what the words meant before a glorious confusion swept away her thoughts in an epiphany. She could not reply because she was unable to do so.

"I don't understand. What will happen to you?" The question seemed a trivial one, but everything, now, hid behind a veil of confusion.

"Nothing." The words were spat out as if to enforce his desperate plight.

"Where will you go?"

"I've no idea. Every law in the universe says I should not exist but, as you can see, I do. As an act of imagination given life, I should imagine I will remain forever as I am. Only time will change the way others perceive me but, like all acts of the imagination, I cannot die." The words seemed calm and reflective.

"This is just too strange to contemplate! How can you be real? If I hadn't read about you in my brother's journal, I should think you nothing more than a hallucination. Maybe you are. Here, let me touch you." Lillian moved toward Sebastian and extended her arm until the tips of her fingers brushed against his arm "You are real! I can't believe it! What will happen to you? Will you change? Age?"

"Age? Yes. Change? No. I will doubtless remain as your brother thought of me. He moves with me for I am a part of him."

"But my brother is *dead*." Lillian tried to emphasise the last word.

"No! No! No!" For the first time, Lillian understood Sebastian's desperation. If he were immortal, and a creation of the mind then he had no-one. He would never grow old with the people he loved. Given that her brother was dead, Sebastian would always be as he was at this moment in time. She tried to convince herself of the impossibility of the situation, yet in front of her stood a creation of the mind! Before she could organise her thoughts, however, Sebastian interrupted: "I must go", he said. Evidently, he had been considering his condition as much as Lillian had been. He swiftly turned, walked through the gate, and disappeared into the gloom.

The rest of the day Lillian spent, as had quickly become her custom, in the old house. Her encounter with Sebastian haunted her imagination. Trying to think of other things, she sought to make the house hers by stamping her identity upon it: hanging a painting here; arranging a plant there, whilst all the while feeling something of an intruder. "I've no right to be here," she would tell herself. By the end of the day, her encounter with Sebastian felt like nothing more than a dream. How could a *person* be a creation of the *mind*? Not only that, one that would never age or die? No, it must have been a dream even if something told her it was not. Perhaps she and her brother had inherited some madness? No, it was too awful to consider.

A few days later the last of her father's financial affairs had been set in order. Lillian, therefore, now had an income that would sustain the employment of a few domestic employees. In such a large house, she would also appreciate the company. With other people in the house, she might also be able to forget Sebastian, whatever he was.

After placing an advertisement in a local newspaper there came a response: a husband and wife applied for the post of gardener and cook. As theirs were the only applications, the posts were duly filled.

They had been expected at nine in the morning, but by ten o'clock the couple had failed to arrive. Lillian busied herself, looking for their arrival at the window. At ten, there was a loud knock on the door. Lillian knew it to be them. Moments later, and with the door now unbolted, her new employees stood in front of her.

The man was typical of many other Welsh characters of the time: his clothes were some years' out of date, yet considered practical; he was rather short, with thick, creased fingers that told of many decades of hard work; he looked every day of his sixty years, what with his hunched shoulders and tufted silver hair that he cut himself. Nonetheless, he had a kind face with large, doleful eyes. He loved his wife and the country he seemed such a part of, Lillian could see that.

The woman was large and maternal. She greeted Lillian with a smile, unconsciously flattening out the wrinkles in her navy-blue coat so that she might give a better impression.

Lillian had been busy arranging the couple's accommodation so that the two would have their own living quarters.

"Ah, Mr and Mrs Llewellyn, come in." Lillian tried to make first words as genial as possible but, in actuality, she hated meeting new people.

"Thank you, Miss." The woman's voice was soft. An accent of the borders rather than the harder tones to the west.

"Please, call me Lillian," the young woman said, bidding the pair enter. Lillian hoped that the two would not yet be familiar with the rumours surrounding the house. As is typical of any Welsh town an elaborate embroidery had been woven over the facts until the rumoured events had become so far removed from the actual ones as to bear no resemblance whatsoever to what had actually happened. Lillian chose not to offer explanations until explanations were sought.

They trailed down a long corridor in awkward silence until Lillian drew them to a halt, opening a door to her left.

"These will be your rooms. I've tidied them up a bit for you but they haven't been used for years so you may have to open a few windows. I'm afraid they're not in the best of repair." Lillian smiled, nervously.

Mr Llewellyn dropped his suitcase to the floor and sighed.

"Home is home though it's never so homely," he said, making his way to a window and opening it. His wife also seemed to visibly relax in her new surroundings. Lillian, for her part, watched the old man struggle with the window before it eventually opened and a cool breeze entered the room.

"Now, if you're to call me Lillian, I hope I can call you both by your first names," The old man still had his back to the two women so Lillian addressed her comments to the woman.

"Yes. I'm Florrie. He's Ivor." His name being mentioned, Ivor awoke from a reverie and turned to see why his name had been spoken. No-one seemed to be expecting a response from him so he turned back to the open window and the garden.

"Well, I hope my home will be your home." Lillian was unsure of how to conduct herself in a situation in which she was in control.

"I hope so. I'll be glad to get away from that town. Only last night, someone was seen digging in the cemetery at gone midnight and then, when he was disturbed, ran off. Anyhow, seems as though he was filling in a grave rather than digging one. All the same,

I'm glad to be away." She looked to her husband, hoping he would validate her story, but he appeared not to be listening as his eyes were still trained on the garden.

"Yes, well I'm sure you'll want to unpack and make yourself at home." Lillian looked at the couple's meagre possessions.

"I'm expecting a housemaid at any moment, so if I can leave you to it." With that, she glided to the door and was gone.

Flo Llewellyn was not concerned that Lillian had cut her chatter dead. She had done nothing more than idly gossip in an effort to hide her insecurity with her new employer. She had not registered what she had been saying until it dawned on her that, perhaps, Lillian had left when she had heard mention of cemeteries. She had almost forgotten the rumours she had heard about Lillian's family and how many of them now lay, it was supposed, silently beneath the cold ground. Now, feeling tactless, her face burned with embarrassment.

Lillian walked from the house to the garden. The old woman's words came back, like an echo in the night. She had not taken offence at what had been said, nor even thought about her own family. What intrigued Lillian was who it might have been in that windswept place, quarrying a grave by moonlight. Who had wished to lay their hands upon a cold corpse at such an hour, and for what reason? As one thought collided into another, her imagination came back to Sebastian. At first, the graveyard incident and that uneasy young man appeared unconnected. Why, then, had she connected them? Of course, the two thoughts might have been entirely arbitrary - as thoughts often are - having no connection to one another whatsoever other than the fact that she had thought them. Something, however, told her that there had to be a connection between Sebastian and the figure in the graveyard. Had it really been Sebastian in that infernal place at such an hour? Surely not! He wouldn't, would he? Then it came to her: the horrifying thought that Sebastian, doubting her word, had gone to exhume her brother's body. No, it was too awful to contemplate. Nonetheless, if anyone were capable of such an act, Lillian thought, it would be him.

As Lillian crossed the sun-drenched grass her attention was captured by a movement near to the gate. Even though she had only seen the figure once before already it was one that she recognised. Out of the shadows stepped Sebastian. Now, as if history were about to repeat itself, they faced one another as they had when first they met.

"Was it you?" Lillian spoke the words quietly. So many things seemed incommunicable between the two, yet so many things could be left unsaid.

"Yes." Sebastian's reply was flat and devoid of emotion.

"What were you thinking? What sort of a monster are you? Must you make everyone else's existence as wretched as your own?" Lillian felt her anger rising. She wanted to hit him - to beat her fist against him - but her own bitter experiences told her that violence was no recourse.

"I loved him. I loved him and I destroyed him. His death gave me a life independent of him, but what sort of a life is it when that life is outside time? For all eternity I must carry the weight of knowing it was I who brought about his death. Can't you understand? I had to know if he were truly dead to know what my future 'wretched existence' holds for me." All the while Sebastian spoke, his gaze had not once averted from Lillian nor had his voice been anything other than low and hoarse.

"But Sebastian, he's been dead for over a year." Lillian's anger began to subside. No longer did she have the wish to punish, or even admonish.

"Yes, and in peace. What peace can I know, knowing it was I that put him beneath the cold clay?" Sebastian's voice betrayed a quiver of emotion.

"What peace can *you* know? What peace can I know, knowing my brother and I harboured feelings for one another in a way we should not? Thank goodness neither of us had acted upon those feelings. Who else but a brother could love someone as wretched and as I? What burden of guilt do you think I carry, knowing my brother and father killed one another because of me? That is a sorrow that can only cease when I cease." Lillian turned away, her voice choking with emotion. Unseen by her companion, sunlight caught her tears, giving them an iridescence.

"Others could love you, Lillian, if only they were given the chance," Sebastian spoke the words with soft hesitation.

"Who? Who could love me now?" Lillian brought herself around to face the young man. Curiosity shone through the tears bedewing her eyes. Her dark hair fell around her face catching the salty course and darkening a few strands.

"You forget. I am your brother or, at least, a part of him. The things he loved and despised, I love and despise. Lillian ... I could love you." Sebastian's sentence seemed to pause the moment for an eternity so that it hung in the air like frozen gossamer. Lillian wanted to throw herself into his arms but the act would have been too impulsive and desperate: the act of a drowning woman clutching nothing more than the tiniest of branches. How would such an act be right when so many things were wrong? He was uncomfortably close to her, yet still she doubted his reality. Perhaps, like her brother, she had invented a character able to fulfil all her darkest, unacknowledged desires. Was there real blood in his veins? But what had he said? To kiss him now would be to kiss a brother. His lineaments and aspect were too like her own. She hated herself and, in hating herself, hated him.

"You must go." Lillian's full lips mouthed the words, almost inaudibly.

"Lillian." Her name was spoken plaintively, almost apologetically.

"Please ... go." Lillian had broken her gaze and looked to the ground. Even the whisper she could manage was tremulous. If Sebastian were to ask her again, her next response would have found all her resolve weaken. She would then have had to admit her feelings to herself, and to him.

"Do you really want me to go?" That was the question Lillian had dreaded. She closed her eyes in an effort to contain her tears and nodded her acquiescence. A silence ensued. Opening her eyes, Lillian was alone.

"Miss?" A soft gentle voice behind Lillian begged her attention. "Miss, I've come about the job."

Lillian swallowed and took out a handkerchief to dry her eyes. What sort of an impression must she have given her prospective employee, standing alone in the middle of her garden, sobbing? She did not wish to appear ridiculous, nor did she wish to fan the flames of local gossip. She had heard the rumours that to live in the old house turned a person mad: what had her actions, seemingly, proven?

"Ah yes, let's go to the house." Lillian led the way. The young woman, she had glanced at for just a second, seemed personable enough. Pretty, one might say although, like Lillian, the young woman thought herself quite the opposite. She also looked to be about the same age as Lillian. Yet Gwen - for that was her name - had known nothing of the tragedy that can blight a young life, just as a cruel wind twists a tree. Gwen's family had been a loving and caring one which, despite their poverty, had made Gwen a woman with a happy disposition.

Happy, that is until she began work at the old house. As the weeks turned to months Gwen became a confidant, as well as a maid, yet all the while her once healthy complexion grew more and more pale. Her once bright eyes became glassy and lifeless. Lillian noticed the malady afflicting her fiend, and the general unhappiness stalking her everywhere she went. Lillian blamed herself: always, she felt people's unhappiness to originate with her. One day, as Gwen cleaned the drawing-room, Lillian waylaid her.

"Gwen, sit down." Lillian gently took her friend by the arm and guided her toward a large tapestry settee that was the centrepiece of the room. All around them the evidence of Gwen's work gleamed. Against the wall, the old furniture shone like ripe horse-chestnuts. Upon it, silverware caught the rays of the sun so that previously dark corners of the room were dappled in flowing colours.

"Gwen, are you happy here?" There was genuine concern in Lillian's voice.

"Yes, I am." Initially, it had seemed as though Gwen were about to pause but after a moment's reflection, in which she looked heavenward as if seeking divine inspiration, the pause furnished her with a curt reply that explained very little.

"Are you *really*? You don't seem happy. I worry about you. Although I would miss you dearly, if you were to leave, I should rather you go and be happy than stay and be so sad." Lillian placed her hand on her friend's arm.

"Well. I'm not unhappy *here*, but I am unhappy." Gwen looked awkward, like a shy suitor telling his sweetheart of his love.

"I guessed you were." Lillian congratulated herself on being so perceptive.

"It's not my job. I love what I do", she quickly responded, before hesitatingly adding "It's you."

"Me?" Lillian could not help sounding shocked. The fact that she made a friend unhappy in some way confirmed all the fears she had about herself. Now, she wanted to laugh; to cry; to throw her arms around Gwen and thank her for confirming what she had always felt about herself: that she could do nothing save pollute the lives of those around her. Gwen, however, was becoming tearful.

"It's just that you seem to have everything and are still so unhappy. It's made me think that, for all my life, when I thought that to have all that you have would have made me completely happy. I've now realised that, even if I did, I might be no happier than I am now. I've always had nothing except the consolation that, in my sad moments, if I had such and such I would be happier. That's not the case, is it? You have everything and are the unhappiest person I know. Seeing you sad makes me sad because I know there is nothing I can do." Gwen's eye focused on the face in front of her.

Denial

"Oh, Gwen! Then you don't hate me." Lillian threw her arms around her friend.

"Hate you? No! You're my best friend." Gwen was astonished to think her words could have been so misunderstood.

"Well Gwen, I may appear to have everything but you've got something money can't buy - a family that loves you. I would trade everything I own to love and be loved. To be as happy as you were when you first came to this place. That must be glorious!" There was no trace of self-pity in Lillian's voice. She spoke the words calmly; comfortingly.

After the two women had finished their conversation, Lillian was left alone. As Gwen finished her chores, Lillian had time to reflect. The sight of Gwen's misery had troubled her for weeks. Now, she felt guilty that she should have caused it although the knowledge that someone cared about her so much gave Lilian a warm glow. Perhaps she should go and look for her friend, hold her tightly, and tell her how much her concern meant. Then again, maybe a second, less spontaneous, show of affection might invite a rebuff that would leave her feeling vulnerable. Gwen's affection was the closest thing Lillian had ever had to an unconditional love. Gwen expected nothing, unlike others who had spoken of love but only used it as a weapon.

"Love comes in different forms. Love can be one friend caring for another. Never think you're not loved",

Gwen had said. Like a trebuchet, it had broken Lillian's defences. An almost inaudible rap at the door announced Gwen's return.

"Gwen, come and sit with me awhile. Forget the house for today." Lillian's friend smiled and made her way to the settee where Lillian sat, waiting.

"I have to be honest, Gwen. I just don't know what it is to love." Lillian's admission startled them both. Lillian, because she had never been able to trust anyone enough to be so candid; Gwen, because she found it hard to believe that anyone as beautiful as her friend should be unloved.

"I didn't know anything of romantic love either. I love my family, but a passion for which I could die has always been denied me. Since I've been working here, a man I've known for a few years, and who I thought never liked me, has asked me to marry him. I don't know what to tell him because I feel little for him. Maybe I do love him and this is what love feels like. I've wanted to tell you, but I didn't want you to worry about my problems when you seemed to have so many of your own." Gwen looked crestfallen as she spoke, her forehead creasing with confusion.

"Oh Gwen, you never said!" Despite everything, Lillian still idealised love, according it the power to transform everything. "Who is he?"

"Well. I've known him for a few years but, as I said, he's never shown any interest until recently. My family has always been poor, whilst his are in insurance and well off. We've always spoken. Maybe he didn't like me because I didn't work. He has a good job and works hard. I know his family lost a lot of money after that mining accident last year so, maybe, he also has his problems."

"I would like to meet him." Lillian gave a positive affirmation as if to negate Gwen's lack of enthusiasm.

"Yes, he wants to meet you." Gwen's voice trailed away into silence as if her thoughts were elsewhere.

"Me?" Lillian was surprised that anyone should wish to seek out her company. Her face flushed.

"Yes. He speaks of you often. I thought you may have known him." Whatever it was Gwen had been thinking had obviously been dismissed and she now accorded Lillian her full attention.

"No. I don't know anyone really." Lillian failed to realise the implication of what she had said.

"That is strange." Gwen frowned.

"I agree. That really is very strange."

*   *   *

Despite Lillian having banished Sebastian, he had not gone far. He had kept his presence out of sight but something tied him to the house. There was the promise made to his friend; then there was Lillian. He would never be able to leave the house completely for he and the house were too tightly bound for that, but what about Lillian? She was the only thing that could change his existence into that of a life worth living.

Sebastian's days were spent wandering. Sometimes his journeys would take him to the bleak and barren wilderness of Mid-Wales where the huge, open vistas - like an empty sheet of music - allowed a vivid imagination such as his to compose its own symphony. Here was a scenery where *anything* might be possible. Often, amid the coarse grass and shattered boulders a solitary, twisted tree would grow; he would smile, thinking it as weatherworn and alone as he. Other times he walked the great valleys, where mountains rose up on all sides like the walls of a giant's tomb, walls that threatened to cascade down upon him in mighty earthen torrents sending him back to hell. On days that were less bleak - days when his terrible isolation was less painful - he would walk to the more lush, pastoral east. Here there seemed to be unity and harmony in the world yet, always alone, he remained outside such holy communion. Here, nonetheless, he might find a poet writing some reverie to a ruined abbey, or eulogising nature. Sebastian, too, found solace in nature even if nature spurned him. Nonetheless, there could be no escape. However far his lonely wanderings took him, he could never stay away from the one place he'd felt tied to for too long. Always there would be a point of recoil. Whilst there was still hope he, at least, could never turn away completely.

Denial

Back in the small town, Sebastian trudged along the dirty streets. Since the death of his friend he could never sleep for sleep, like death, was also denied him. Slowly, he walked, for having nowhere to go, he had become aimless. Every street was quiet. Every street, that is, except the streets of the town that had once led to a dock. Here, fights were breaking out as landlords sought their beds and crowds were beginning to empty into the streets. Sebastian withdrew into a darkened doorway. The prospect of an encounter with *any* member of the human race was bad enough but tonight it would be unbearable.

In the gloom, Sebastian could see but not be seen. Voices approached. Two of the multitude whose drink-soaked bodies staggered upon the road that, moments before, Sebastian's aching frame had traversed.

"No, you can't do it." Despite the slurred tones, the words were distinct.

"Why?" A voice as equally slurred as the first broke into a laugh, a laugh only friends have about a secret collusion. In the darkness, flashing eyes were watching their every move and ears listening to their intoxicated ramblings. The two figures continued to walk, propping each other up until they came to a halt before the bright window of their next inn.

The first of the two men stood at almost Sebastian's height. His features, however, were remarkably different. His face was long and thin and appeared to have been squeezed into an awkward shape. His lips - even from a distance - were markedly thin and to such a degree that his face, far from having a mouth, appeared to have nothing more than a split beneath his nose.

"What do I get, then?" The thin lips pulled apart like a bloodless slash.

"Oh, you'll be alright, don't you worry." Once again, the laughter between the two flared up like fire beneath a bellows.

Sebastian turned his attention to the second figure. He was, perhaps, slightly shorter than the first but of a heavier and more athletic build. His mouth was coarse, suggesting a permanent look of disdain. He, like his friend, appeared uncommonly well dressed for the little town.

"But how ... how ... how are you going to do it?" In his stupor, he appeared to have forgotten the second half of his sentence until with all his concentration, it came back to him. "How?" The one with thin lips was evidently not satisfied with the time it was taking his friend to respond, feeling it necessary to ask the question again.

"I know. I heard you the first time. I was just thinking." The heavier of the two leaned against the window and, fumbling in his frockcoat pocket, removed his empty hands a few seconds later. He stared at them in confusion, trying to remember what he had been looking for, or what he had lost.

"And?"

"And? Oh, I've shown some interest in that girl that's working for her. Gwen something. I don't know ... I don't know *anything* anymore!" The two broke into laughter and embraced one another as only two drunks can.

"Gwen Davis?" The taller of the two, it appeared, was marginally less drunk.

"Is that it? Yes, I think you're right." The confusion he had found in looking at his hands was now transferred to his friend's face. He looked up, frowned and squinted, then smiled as the face came into focus.

"And?" Although the questions kept coming, the tone in which they were asked suggested no real interest, only idle curiosity.

"Well, she thinks I like her. I've tried to get myself an invite to meet her boss. Lillian is it? From there, what could be easier? She's got no friends, a lot of money, so a seduction shouldn't be too difficult."

Checking himself, Sebastian stood silently in the shadows and hoped the two would let slip further plans.

"But she's a hysteric. I've heard it was her who got her brother to kill her father." The words were said as if some great secret had been told and enforced with a wink, ludicrous in his state, as both eyes closed.

"They're just stories. I know that one because I started it!" The two broke into laughter for the third time.

Sebastian felt a cold rage run through him before it turned to a flame. His large eyes watched the two figures steady themselves before they stumbled off. What to do? The thought that some buffoon thought himself conniving and irresistible enough to wield his duplicitous charm upon two women with the sole aim of lining his pocket ate into Sebastian. He tried to control his anger, realising that it was born of jealousy, and from such a genesis something might irrevocably escalate. It wasn't that Lillian could not take care of herself as she could. She had proven herself an able and capable woman on more than one occasion. No, Sebastian knew all the pain Lillian had suffered in her short life and how much damage the actions of the self-serving imbecile he had just heard speaking would cause. He felt honour-bound to prevent further grief if it were in his power to do so.

With stealth, he crept from his dark dominion and into the grey night. The pair had disappeared into the hungry jaws of the town; it was up to Sebastian to follow. He knew the two would be negotiating a lane through the churchyard, somewhere he could hide. There, under the high steeple that had never offered him salvation, he could eschew prayer for prey. For the first time ever, the church had shown Sebastian a way. In the jaws of the night, shapes were threatening, like dead things awaking from slumber.

Almost at the point of invisibility the two figures that, unbeknown to them, were now being hunted paused before going their separate ways. Now Sebastian could pounce! Slowly, the drunken braggadocio swayed his way home. Sebastian moved swiftly and with purpose, the final words of the two still reverberating in his ears. Sebastian and his quarry crossed the bridge that divided the town. The wind had lashed the silent murky depths beneath them into a foaming tempest that snarled like an angry animal. Almost within striking distance, yet with still no plan of attack, Sebastian knew he would rely on instinct, just as he had always done.

Despite the weather, the click of the footsteps of the figure in front upon the pavement, and the rustle the dried leaves made as he dragged his feet through them could now be clearly heard. Drink had benumbed the senses of the hunted so that he, at least, considered himself alone. With one final movement, Sebastian drew alongside and, with a firm grip upon the man's arm, pulled him around.

"What the ...?" In his drunken state, he fell to the floor.

"I want a word with you." Sebastian kneeled down and leaned over the prostrate figure, drawing his face near.

"Who are you, then?" There was no tinge of fear in the voice, only aggression.

"That doesn't concern you. I'm a friend of Lillian's. Stay away." The words were spoken with venomous intent.

"I don't know any Lillian. I don't know what you're talking about." Turning his head away, the drunken figure lashed out with the back of his arm. It was met with outstretched fingers that caught the flailing arm firmly by the wrist, before squeezing tightly.

"Oh God, it's not me! I think my friend knows a Lillian." For the first time, clouds that had veiled the pair in darkness had drawn aside like stage curtains; now the pair were bathed in a pallid limelight. For the first time, the light was bright enough to catch the pitiless depths of Sebastian's angry eyes, eyes that focussed on the now trembling clown beneath him.

How did such a figure as Sebastian know so much about him? Fear had a sobering effect and now he asked himself how a stranger had come by his information. What were his motives? Perhaps *he* also wanted to get his hands on the young woman's money.

"Look, if it's the money, maybe we can work something out." Sebastian raised a hand to strike the cowering form beneath him, but his glance was fearful enough.

"Oh God, I know who you are! Please, don't kill me." Something deep within the young man's intoxicated brain had started to work. Like everyone in the town, he had heard of the increasingly diabolic nature of Lillian's brother. Had that diabolism succeeded in raising the Devil? To a superstitious mind, it seemed possible. Like all gossip, it had become misshapen and magnified a story until nothing of the truth remained. In the pious, twisted little community, had what had once been suggested, now been confirmed? "You ... You keep away from me. I know what you are! It was you that killed the others. Kill her as well, I'll not stop you, just don't kill me."

"I'll not kill you." Sebastian's voice was calm. He allowed himself a smile, realising the insensible idiot thought him the Devil incarnate!

"What then?" Sebastian had regained his composure. A passion too excessive might have caused untold harm and that was not what he wanted. The temporary respite was enough for the young, still prone, man to take an opportunity to regain his liberty. Seeking to free himself, he began to flail wildly about, but Sebastian's grip was too strong. How could he free himself? How to escape with body *and* soul intact? With his free arm, he reached into an inside pocket of his long dark coat. Sebastian anticipated what was to come as the hand withdrew. In the moonlight, the blade shone like a mirror in the noonday sun. Sebastian took a step backwards.

Blade outstretched, the drunk lunged forward, only to lose his footing and fall. In the mottled, flickering light, a dark and rapidly widening patch now contrasted with the brilliance of his white shirt. Moonlight caught the dark stream, making it glisten. Embedded in the chest of the still shape beneath him, Sebastian could only see the protruding handle. The blade had sunk to the hilt in the soft, drunken, flesh. A fearful and ghastly groan emerged from the mouth of the victim, heightened by a guttural rattle deep within his throat. As the patch of blood expanded, Sebastian crouched beside the injured man. Carefully, he dipped his fingers in the life flow before bringing them to his lips. 'So that's what death tastes like,' he told himself. Already the hot effusion had cooled and was now beginning to coagulate.

"Murder! You'll not get away with this." The whisper was fearful and breathless. The look of disdain Sebastian had observed a little earlier was now a sneer.

"Look, shut up and I'll help you." Sebastian brought his face near to the other man's. He hadn't wanted to help him, yet found himself unable to let him die alone in a gutter.

"Murder!" In the distance, footsteps were approaching. What to do? Stay and be accused? Or go, and make good his escape from a crime of which he was innocent? Footsteps were coming nearer. One more "Murder!" would surely bring help. Sebastian arose. Despite it being autumn, he was, in an instant, lost in the still dense foliage afforded by the trees that stood, shaking, on either side of the lane. Voices drew nearer. He would be safe, but what of he who had been left? He had gone horribly silent. Then there was a groan.

"What was that?" One of the approaching figures had heard the noise.

"Don't know. An animal?" Both voices were slurred, yet laden with panic the pitch of their voice beginning to rise.

"What's that?" From his haven, Sebastian guessed that one of the two had located the source of their unease.

"Christ, it's a body!" Suspicions were confirmed. There followed the sound of a few hurried footsteps that seemed as anxious as the voices had sounded a few moments before. They too were interrupted by a long, deeper, groan. "Oh God, he's bleeding!"

"Bleeding? He's been stabbed!"

"Who did this, boy?"

"The Devil! The Devil did it!" The voice was gasping, punctuated by gulps of air. Less audible than the other two, he sounded desperately ill.

Sebastian allowed himself a smile. He knew that he, at least, would be safe. Who would believe a drunk claiming to have been stabbed by the Prince of Darkness himself? Silently, Sebastian slipped away.

Lillian was never far from Sebastian's thoughts, yet the events of the night made him more acutely aware of their separation from one another than ever. He had not intended to return to the house since her banishment, but tonight was different. He had to be near her, even if it only meant to walk a path that she might have walked.

With a purpose he alone accorded it, Sebastian made his way back to the old house and its garden, his journey lit by the silvered countenance of Diana, her loving arrows piercing his upturned face. The coldness of the night had given rise to a mist that clung in frozen abandon all around him. Within an hour, he was standing beneath Lillian's window. A solitary flame flickered in the darkness. How he longed to make his presence known. To take her in his arms so that she, with a few soft words, might make everything right. But Lillian had banished him: he could never let her know he was still near to her, at least not until he was sure that is where she wanted him.

The next morning, Lillian's old gardener arose early. The autumn season gave him plenty of work, not least of which was the many leaves to be raked. He did not trade in the same sort of gossip as his wife, but that was because he had fewer friends than she. She kept him well informed on all the local rumours, especially the ones regarding the house in which they lived.

Now that summer was over and the season of mellow fruitfulness was upon them, the lawn needed less tending. The old man sighed. He had been a gardener all his life, and had always enjoyed his work but, just occasionally, thought how different his life might have been had he been given opportunities. He bent down and pulled up a fern whose knotty roots, deeply embedded in the Welsh hillside, reminded him of his own life.

Ah well, it was too late to do anything to change his life now. From the corner of his eye, something caught his attention. Somewhere near the gate, in the early morning sun, something had moved.

"Ah, it's just a breeze", he told himself, but hadn't that wind come from the east? The old man used proverbs to give some order to his existence. Now, a proverb came back to him: 'When the wind is in the east, 'tis neither good for man nor beast.' He gave an involuntary shudder, remembering his wife's stories.

"Ah, it *has* to be the wind." This time he spoke the words aloud, in the hope of feeling less alone. To hear the sound of his own voice gave him a feeling of support. But what if spoken words had only drawn attention when otherwise he might not have been noticed? He began to wonder. Again, a branch moved but this time there could be no mistaking it for an effect of the weather. Something awful and foreboding was lurking; watching. Trying to dismiss his fears, the old man began to rake the dead leaves that had fallen in the night.

A rusting creak as cast iron ground against cast iron told the old gardener that the gate had opened, or had been opened. Dare he look? Lifting his gaze, he squinted. Within a second, a dark silhouette had become clear and distinct.

Taking a step backwards, the old man's legs became entangled with his rake and he stumbled. Quickly, he brought himself around: if an attack were imminent, he wanted to be ready.

If Llewellyn had expected to see something alien, he found it in the features of Sebastian, whose bearing set him so apart from others in the little community. Instinct told the old man to run, but try as he might he could not avert his eyes. As the old man blinked, the figure was gone. All that remained was a clump of bushes. Beyond, the gate swung.

Denial

All that day there remained, it seemed, an unearthly presence in the garden. Nervously, the old man tried to work, all the while feeling as if a pair of cold and unblinking eyes appraised his every move. Now it seemed as though something awful had descended over the garden. Had what once had happened in the house come back to haunt it?

The working day drew to a close. After carefully tidying away his tools, the old man returned to the house. After a pause, he considered that tonight he would lock away his tools, thinking it a sensible precaution given that axes and scythes were amongst them. As he ascended the steps to the back door, his wife came out to greet him.

"You look as though you've seen a ghost, love." Her voice as warming as winter mead.

"It's nothing. 'Talk of the Devil and he is bound to appear'." He tried to make what he said sound light and humorous, but his wife knew him too well. She recognised the underlying disquiet.

"Pardon?" She was curious, but not excessively so. She raised her hand to his face, sliding it across his cheek, and into his hair.

"Just someone in the garden earlier. A strange-looking fella. I think he must have been homeless. 'If the eyes are the window of the soul', he must be a lonely wanderer searching for his, because he certainly didn't have one when I saw him."

Despite his earlier conviction not to speak of his

experience, now that he had started there could be no stopping him.

"Didn't you get him off the place?" The old woman felt concerned; threatened.

"Didn't have a chance to, dear. 'Quickly come, quickly go'." The old man sat down upon a bench embedded in the wall of the deep porch and crossed his legs, before beginning to untie his bootlaces.

"Then why did you say 'Devil'?" Flo Llewellyn sat opposite her husband, before placing her hands in her lap.

"Oh, I don't know." He tried to shrug off the conversation as though it were trivial and did not warrant so much attention. Both knew this not to be the case, but the old woman took the hint and let the matter drop. What neither had seen was Lillian approaching from within the house. She had only caught the last part of the conversation, but it was enough. Given that it was her garden, she didn't feel it unmannerly, or an imposition, to ask of whom they had been speaking.

"Ivor, excuse me for interrupting, but did you say there was someone in the garden today?" Unexpected, Lillian's voice startled the old couple.

"Yes, Miss." The old man pulled off a boot, before continuing with the next.

"Where?" Lillian braced herself by leaning, apparently nonchalantly, against a wall.

"By the gate." The words seemed to resound, like an echo. Lillian held her breath, lest her companions realise the significance of what had just been said.

"Why did you call him the 'Devil'?" Lillian was still unsure whether it was Sebastian who had returned. The words made the old man blanch. His job might be in jeopardy if Lillian thought he was spreading rumours.

"It's just me, Miss. As they say: 'One man may steal a horse, while another may not look over a hedge'. I didn't like the look of him from the start." The old man stopped untying his boots and, with his sad eyes, looked at Lillian.

"Well then, Ivor, I don't want you repeating this story to anyone. We all know how these things can take on a life of their own." Lillian had no wish to chastise the old man for, in actuality, he had made her very happy by suggesting that there was the possibility that Sebastian had returned. The old man closed his eyes, drew down the corners of his mouth, and nodded. Her secret would be safe. Lillian turned to go, yet some deep instinctive urge stayed her moving.

"Ivor, this figure. Did you notice anything unusual about him?" Lillian's voice betrayed her curiosity. The old couple both looked up at her.

"Yes, and no." The reticence in his voice betrayed his uncertainty.

"What?" Lillian asked, as Flo looked to her husband, then back to Lillian. Ivor pulled a face as he struggled for the right words. Lillian knew then that Sebastian had returned. "Thank you." Trying to regain her composure, she turned before walking speedily to the inner sanctuary of the house.

No more was said about the mystery that evening. The next day, as Gwen arrived for work, Lillian noticed her friend's red eyes and swollen cheeks.

"Whatever's the matter, Gwen?" Lillian took her friend by the arm and led her from the hall into a nearby sitting room. Knowing of her friend's genuine compassion for her allowed Lillian to reciprocate a similar sentiment.

"Do you remember I told you someone had asked me to marry him? Well, he's been attacked." The young woman began to sob, allowing herself to slump into a nearby chair.

"Oh God, that's awful! When did this happen? Do they know who did it?" Lillian fell gently to her knees at Gwen's feet, before pressing Gwen's hands into her own. Lillian's long dark hair cascaded into Gwen's lap. Her dark eyes looked on, concerned.

"I don't know. Nobody can get any sense from him." Gwen closed her eyes, but some image must have flickered across her mind, for soon her chest began to heave and she exploded into tears. "I don't know how anyone could harm him as he hasn't an unkind bone in his body. The doctors think he might die. It's made me realise that I *do* love him, now there's a chance I might lose him."

"Gwen, what has he said has happened?" Gwen had become the sister Lillian had never had. Gently squeezing Gwen's hands, she tried to coax the information from her.

"Some men found him stabbed and bleeding, in the road. He can't say anything about who did it. He was drunk, and now he has a fever and is imagining all sorts. Nobody knows what happened. Oh God, what will I do if he dies?" With that, the young woman broke into new convulsions.

"Now look, you'll be alright. You try and think who would want to kill him." Without the emotional involvement, Lillian was able to take a more practical approach.

"There's no-one. No-one. That's why they're saying he tried to kill himself. Everyone's saying his family is one step away from the workhouse and that that is why he did it."

By now, the words had become lost on Lillian. Sebastian's face had come back to haunt her. Since first she met him, she had felt him capable of any atrocity. He was wild; untamed. But there was more, much more. In Sebastian, Lillian had found the voice of her own soul. Was that why she found him so attractive yet, at bottom, frightening? He had a vengeful streak, she felt sure, but Gwen's story had triggered a flow of ideas that now crowded in on her.

"Go to him, Gwen. Take as much time as you need. Just keep me informed." Lillian had snapped out of her cloud of thought. She had not wanted to think Sebastian capable of such things, because it suggested she too might be capable of such an act.

"Oh, thank you!" In an instant, Gwen had put her coat and hat back on, and was gone. Lillian stood in silence as her friend's footsteps quickly pattered away. She was now alone, the Llewellyns far removed in other parts of the house. After a few minutes, she moved toward the window. Rolling and angry clouds were gathering with alarming speed upon the horizon. A deep rumble, that could be felt as much as heard, preceded an awful blue-white flash that cracked like a cruel whip across the sky. On the distant hills, a single tree stood blasted, its barren branches aflame.

Lillian knew Sebastian had returned. Lillian stared from the window, pensive; vacant. Her soul, like an empty chalice waiting to be filled; her gaze wandering over the dark farmhouses in the distance. Was it really night already? The black sky indicated so. How long had she stood there, lost in a realm of thoughts unique to her and her experience? A minute? An hour? A day?

Tiny rivulets flooded down the pane of glass that separated Lillian from the storm outside. Out there, there was nothing only the blackness of the eternal void. Only Sebastian could fill that aching chasm for only he had made her painfully aware of it.

Thunder growled in the distance, slow and indistinct as if two mighty worlds were in collision. Then, another strike of the white whip as lightning again seemed to lash at some recalcitrant enemy. Some thought the brilliance capable of re-animating life. This time, it only illuminated it. Had that been a figure, far below her, in the outer reaches of the garden? A second flash confirmed her suspicions. There, far below the window, stood Sebastian, his face beaten by the deluge. Silently, he watched her form in the window high above him.

Lillian gave a gasp. Sebastian's features had an uncomfortable familiarity to them. In the savage storm, he seemed different to how she remembered him. Now, his face had a frail, haunted, beauty to it that frightened her. Guilt came in torrents, like the rain upon her true love's face. Somehow, she felt responsible for his trouble.

It would be foolish to ask him inside. A situation might arise that she would not be able to control. She knew Sebastian would never hurt her: it was her own feelings she sought to imprison. Moving from the window to the door she asked herself 'what to do'? She would have to ask him to leave. It would be difficult, but what other recourse was open to her? Reaching for her coat: she would not let herself suffer unduly.

The door was still slightly ajar. Evidently, Gwen had left it open in her haste. Now a damp patch had worked its way through the opening, soaking the cold stone floor. Lillian stepped forth and carefully made her way down the old steps that, even in the light of day, often felt unsafe. Now, she feared falling. Once again, the lightning flashed. This time Lillian could not suppress a scream. Sebastian had come to her. In the light that had momentarily cleaved the hopeless dark, his form stood less than a breath in front of her, his lips almost touching her own; wild eyes searched for an unspoken response.

"Sebastian..." Not a scream, but a breathless whisper. By now, his arm had been placed gently around her waist, the other brought up so that the palm of his hand touched her cheek; his thumb tenderly brushing her lips.

"Lillian." The way he softly spoke her name made her shiver; her knees weaken.

"I thought you had returned. People have been talking." She turned her head to the side and broke free from Sebastian's embrace.

"People do." Sebastian let his arms fall to his side.

"No, talking about *you*. Or, at least, a person I hoped might be you." Lillian had not realised her words had betrayed her true feelings.

"Hoped?" Sebastian had noticed her slip.

"Guessed! I meant guessed." But it was no good as any denial now would be a false one.

All the while, the two figures were becoming saturated, as the rain rolled down the mountainside and into the valley. In the distance, thunder rumbled like a bellowing beast. Aside from the momentary lightning flashes, the two remained in darkness.

"Well, what have they been saying? I may be

guilty of many crimes, but I do have some virtues."

"I never said you didn't." Sebastian was twisting the conversation away from what she had wanted to say. Lillian looked around her. The storm had begun to bear down on her.

"Can you take me somewhere away from here?" She was, after all, just one frail person. How could she match the majestic power of the vast eternal? She now regretted asking, fearing Sebastian might see it as an invitation to enter her house. He did not.

"We can go over there." Sebastian was gesturing toward the gate, and what lay beyond.

"I'm not sure." She didn't fear what lay beyond, as her brother had done. She didn't fear the supernatural: it was what was *natural* that she feared.

"You'll be quite safe, trust me." Without waiting for her reply, Sebastian took Lillian's arm and walked to the entrance. Already his firm grip had softened her resolve. Beneath it, she felt safe. Yes, the place he was taking her to felt forbidden yet only now, as she stood on its threshold, did she realise how delicious forbidden fruits could taste.

"Come with me." Sebastian's hand slipped down her arm until it reached her hand. Slowly his fingers entwined with hers. She wanted to turn and run away; to pull her hand from his and slap his face yet could do neither. She wanted to hit him; to knock him to the ground; to put an end to his immortal being, but knew she *could* not; she also wanted to fall into his arms and press her lips to his, but *dared* not.

In the darkness. Sebastian lit a candle. Its brightness was enough for Lillian to see where she was. Amazed, she found they had already passed through the gate and were now in a dark wood.

In the pale brilliance, Lillian looked to Sebastian. In the little coppice, no rain fell. From somewhere, more and more candles had been brought forth and were now being lit.

"All these candles!" Lillian thought aloud.

"Call me Prometheus!" Sebastian turning, smiled. Lillian sat down and made herself comfortable. It wasn't long before the little copse resembled a Catholic church.

"Sebastian... about my brother's journal." Lillian's voice was soft and low. With the final candle now lit, Sebastian walked to Lillian before kneeling in front of her and taking her hands in his.

"Your brother had a very active imagination." Lillian wanted to pursue the matter but chose not to. Away from the storm, she was beginning to again feel the blood flow within her veins. After a few moments' deliberation, the conversation continued.

"Sebastian, this is wrong." She tried not to look at him, although well aware that he was looking at her.

"What is?" Now he was playing games, she thought.

"Us."

"Why?"

"Because I say it is. It feels as though you're my brother." Under the heat of his attention, she felt herself beginning to redden.

"Brother, or kindred spirit?" His tone was becoming persuasive.

"You're confusing me… in here!" Lillian pulled a hand from his and, clenching it into a fist, banged her chest.

"It doesn't confuse me," Sebastian countered.

"Yes, but you're different."

Sebastian withdrew his hand and, rising to his feet, began to walk to each candle, pinching out the flame with his bare fingers. Only when there were just a few left did he, once again, permit his gaze to fall upon Lillian. By now, his face was dry; his hair, however, still wet, fell about his face.

"So, that's the problem." His voice suggested he had always known the reason. Now, it had merely been confirmed. Under his gaze, Lillian felt her fortitude begin to dissolve and turned away.

"That *is* the problem. I just don't know. I feel as though I know you *too* well, yet another part of me doesn't know you at all. You frighten me. I'm scared to have you near me, yet miss you when you are away. You seem too like me, but I hate myself and in hating myself I can't help but hate you." Lillian longed to lift her eyes, to gauge the reaction her words had provoked but dared not. She listened for a response, but there was none. Should she look? If she caught that gaze - that smile - her uncertainty would magnify tenfold. "Why did you stab that man?" Lillian sought to escape the pain Sebastian had caused her by asking of the pain he had caused another.

"How do you know it was me?" Sebastian showed no trace of guilt: maybe he hadn't been involved, Lillian thought. He sought to avoid answering, knowing he could never lie to Lillian; he could, however, avoid telling the truth.

"Was it you?" Lillian knew a direct question would get a direct answer. A heavy sigh preceded his response.

"Yes, Lillian, it was me." Sebastian turned away from Lillian and placed his hands against a yew tree, bending his head forward as he did so.

"Why did you do it?" Lillian's voice was flat, as she battled to contain her emotions.

"I cannot say."

"Cannot, or will not?"

"Lillian!" Sebastian's response was plaintive.

"Sebastian, I *demand* an answer!"

"It is an answer I cannot give." To tell Lillian that there had been a plan to seduce her solely for her money would be a cruelty beyond measure. No-one had ever loved her for herself. She had trusted Gwen's judgement when she had said her beau was an honest man. Would she believe Sebastian if he were now to unmask that man as a villain? Wouldn't it look as if he were simply blaming another for his own guilt? To tell her that her trust had been ill-founded would open a wound that might never heal. Whatever the consequences, he could never tell her the real reason.

Lillian took the silence as an insult; as though she had been slighted or ignored, which only inflamed her temper.

"Sebastian, will you answer me?" Still, there was no response. "Is it a practice of yours to go around attempting to murder innocent people? After all, you managed to dispose of my brother rather cleverly." As soon as she had said it, Lillian bit her tongue with regret.

Sebastian made no movement, indeed made no response whatsoever. Lillian looked up to see only his back and bowed head. The candle over which he stood spluttered and plunged them into darkness. Tears had filled Sebastian's eyes and, falling to the ground, it had been these that had doused the little flame.

"I'm sorry Sebastian. Please forgive me." The words were barely audible.

"How could you think such a thing? I loved your brother. Maybe I did destroy him, but I didn't murder him. Do you know what it feels like to walk around with a burden of grief and guilt like that upon my shoulders? To exist knowing one of the few people I have ever loved lies rotting away in the cold ground because of my actions? Do you know what it is like to have these thoughts and know that until the end of time they will always be with me? Even after everything else has gone and I alone exist, that knowledge will still haunt me. The knowledge that I could have saved him. And now? What could be worse than a condemnation by she who remains - the sole vessel of my passion? Do you think I would have let him go alone had I known the outcome? All I gave him was the knowledge he needed to act in a way that was true to himself ..." Sebastian's sentence broke and he turned away.

"I'm sorry." Lillian's words sounded hollow and empty. The silence between the two became deafening before Lillian continued. "Sebastian, it's not that I *don't* feel for you - I feel for you *too* much." Sebastian turned to face Lillian, as though simply to hear the words would not have been enough. Lillian, her eyes now accustomed to the light, anticipated the move and turned away. "I worry about you. You say you want us to be together. Maybe it would make us both happy now, but what about in ten years? Twenty years? Fifty years? Sebastian, I'm not like you. There is blood in my veins. This skin will age and wither. How can we two be one when you shall forever remain as you are now? Sebastian, I have to think of what's right for *both* of us."

"No, Lillian." Sebastian made a sudden movement toward her, falling to his knees at her feet. Clutching both her hands, he pressed them to his lips. Tears, again, began to well in his eyes. Teardrops spilt from the corners, trickling warm and wet over Lillian's hands. "Whatever you say, I won't go. I want to always be with you. I cannot leave you."

"Oh, Sebastian!" By now, she too had begun to

cry. "Tell me it isn't so. Tell me the warmth I feel beneath my fingers is the blood of a human heart - that the tears flowing from your eyes are the same as mine own. Tell me that is true and I will try to forget everything else. You don't know how I long to press my lips to yours, but to do so would be my undoing, knowing afterwards they nevermore could part. Sebastian, tell me that the years will not take me from you and that their passing will change us *both*. Tell me, and I will believe you. But, I fear, where now you hold a young woman, one day she will be an old one, whilst you remain as you are now." Her sentence broke off, choked by her tears.

"I don't care. What can my existence be without you?" Sebastian stood and brought his face toward Lillian's until the warmth of his breath touched her face. In silence, Sebastian brought his lips forward, lifting his hand as he did so to draw it through her hair. As their lips were about to touch, Lillian brought the palm of her hand between them and turned away.

"Sebastian, I care. It hurts me more than you can ever know to tell you this, but you *must* leave." Convulsively, Sebastian's grip tightened around a thick mass of Lillian's hair. "Sebastian, you're hurting me!"

"And what are you doing to me? To *us*?" Lillian began to sob profusely. Closing her eyes, she brought a little handkerchief from her pocket and mopped away her tears.

"But Lillian, if you too could live forever, you would never find anyone who loves you more than I."

The desperation in his voice had gone, as he let his hands fall to his side.

"You don't know that." Both of them knew in their heart that he spoke the truth.

"I do because you don't know the depth of my affection." Sebastian extended a hand, in the hope that his touch might console her.

"Nor you, mine. That is why you must leave and never return. Sebastian, ours is a love against nature." Lillian closed her eyes. There was nothing but silence. Lillian guessed that Sebastian had already left. She was about to break into a fresh outburst of uncontrolled sobs when a hand gently, just for a moment, took hold of hers. Through her veil of tears, she could see Sebastian's disconsolate face drawing nearer her own.

"Lillian, please don't send me away. Stop and think about what it will do to both of us. Is it really your dearest wish that I should leave?" Choking back the tears she could do nothing more than nod an affirmation. Was she doing the right thing? Already there were doubts. Would it be right to say yes, and live for the eternal now? But then, what of the future? What would other people say? If she were to follow her passions, then she would fall into his arms here and now. How would it be to run her fingers through his long, dark hair? To press her lips to his? No! She had changed her mind. She must have him or die. Wiping her eyes, she opened them only to find the little wood cold, dark, and empty.

Lillian made a dash back to her garden. If she were quick, she might be able to catch him. Through the gate, the raging storm lashed the Welsh mountainside more terribly than ever. Now, it seemed as if her world were ending. Where was he? Lillian shouted his name at the top of her voice. Why had she sent him away again! Nowhere was Sebastian to be seen. To call his name was futile for it was lost in the roar of the elements. Nature had conspired against her. Slowly, she sank to her knees in the mud.

"Oh Sebastian, I'm sorry. I'm so, *so* sorry. Please come back … I love you." The words were spoken quietly into the sodden earth.

It was too late. Already, the young man had made his way up an ancient mountain path toward what appeared to be an equally old outcrop of farm buildings, seemingly wrought from the landscape and long since abandoned. Oblivious to Lillian's lamentations, onwards he strode, ever onward, out into the hopeless night.

The last few hours of that day Lillian spent in solitude, in the old house. All the while, the weather raged and foamed like a wild, untamed beast. Inside, floods were equally forthcoming as Lillian bewailed her lost love. To think it was she who had cast him out, uncaring of where he might go, not even thinking if he *had* somewhere to go. Then she thought of how she really felt for him, and how, now, he might never know. Would he always think himself scorned when, in actuality, he was adored? Would she be able to treat him lovingly, even if he did return? Then she would think of the possibility of never seeing him again and, once again, the tears flowed.

When Lillian awoke the next morning, the events of the previous day seemed distant; dreamlike, as though they had happened centuries before, or had been nothing more than a story someone had once told, and her imagination had embroidered the rest. She had expected Sebastian's presence to be still felt by the vacuum he had left behind yet today, for the moment, things felt normal.

Pulling back the sheets, Lillian took a few faltering steps toward the window, yawning and trying to shake the last vestiges of sleep from her aching body. In the morning sunshine, the garden appeared brilliant: even her bedroom felt as if golden arms were stretching through the panes, to tenderly enfold her. Despite the day being an autumn one, the garden looked new: fresh.

A gentle knock on her bedroom door begged her attention. Lillian turned, just as Gwen pushed the door open and entered.

"Gwen, you're back!" Lillian ran to her friend and threw her arms around her. The two embraced. Lillian had missed her friend. So much had happened in the short time they had been apart, that Lillian felt as though they had last met a lifetime ago. "How's your intended?"

"Oh, he's much better. The truth has come out.

He'd seen a young woman being attacked by a man and, bravely, went to save her. In the fight that followed he was stabbed. He may have been a bit drunk, but he's so brave." Gwen became starry-eyed, as she looked at the ceiling with a smile on her face.

"Not attacked, then?" In a strange way, she hoped Gwen's fiancé had been attacked. She, after all, had blamed Sebastian. She could feel justly vindicated if the attack had been an unprovoked one perpetrated by Sebastian. Had the injured man not been the victim of an attack, then she had sent Sebastian away for the sole reason that his presence was too much of a temptation to her. But what if Gwen's intended was telling the truth? What if Sebastian had been attacking a woman and he, being genuinely chivalrous, had gone to her assistance? Was Sebastian lying? She loved him and hated him; was jealous of him; would have given him all she had but was such an attack beyond him? If only she could convince herself of his villainy, it might ease the pain of never seeing him again. No! That thought was just too awful. She would lie down and die now if she thought that to be the case. Oh, to see the breeze blow through his hair again, or the light catch the colour of his eyes.

"No, not attacked as such. After his head cleared the truth came out. He cried as he told me how helpless he had felt at not being able to do more to save that woman." Gwen said, in ignorant admiration.

The words seemed to grab Lillian. Before, there

had been uncertainties about whether she had done the right thing in sending Sebastian away. Now, it began to appear that she had been wrong. It had helped to presume him guilty, easing her own doubts. Now, if he were innocent, she felt as if she had betrayed them both.

Gwen set a small silver tray that she had brought upon the heavy oak desk, from which Lillian conducted her limited correspondence, and left. Although her duties were, strictly speaking, to clean the house, the bond that had grown up between the two women meant that she often brought Lillian her breakfast in the morning. Occasionally, the two would have breakfast together but Gwen was evidently busy today.

Now that Lillian was alone, she wandered back to the window. The old gardener was pottering about trying to look busy, but in actuality, doing very little.

"Sebastian ... What have I done? Will, I ever see you again?" She raised her hand to her face and was surprised to find her eyes had moistened her cheeks. Tiny tears streamed between her fingers. A few drops fell upon her hair, unsealing a scent. "Sebastian." Even the aroma of his body clung to her.

Days turned to weeks; weeks to months. Lillian began to reconcile herself to not seeing Sebastian again, yet far from time easing the pain, every day became a trial. Nights were no easier. Lillian went to bed breathing his name; every morning she awoke from dreams of him. Sleep, nonetheless, brought some escape, for it was only then that they could be together.

Tenderly; gently, her fingers would run over the contours of his face. Softly, yet with strength, his arms would hold her close to him, making everything right and safe in the world. All the pain would go. He would tell her how much he loved everything about her, even the things she hated about herself because those things made her uniquely her. She was the person he loved utterly: without condition or fear. Then she would awaken and find herself alone in an otherwise empty room. She would tell herself it had all been a dream - a fantasy - because no-one could ever feel like that about her, not wanting to acknowledge the fact that Sebastian really did feel about her in such a way.

Drearily, every day became the same as the last. Sometimes, she thought of how Sebastian must feel, for sometimes she too felt nature to be mocking her, leaving her an outsider, unable to participate. Why did she feel so bad? After all, she had everything anyone could want: a nice house, money, a friend that loved her. Yet without that special love, it all meant nothing. Only Sebastian could supply that love, and what had she done? Sent him away! It hadn't been anything he had done - even she could recognise that - nor could he have done more. It was her own feelings about herself that had destroyed everything. Feeling unlovable, she had become just that. Every day, she withdrew more and more; hating herself more and more. Looking in the mirror, she would see a monster, where others saw beauty. Who but Sebastian could see it all and still be there for her? Her inward self - the part that blooms like a rare orchid when nourished with love and affection - had died. Inside her there was nothing but dry and dusty sands, awaiting a little rain. Only she could see the many bleached bones upon that sand, bones that had once been living things who had died waiting.

A year slowly slipped by her. Nothing, on the surface, appeared to have changed. Lillian found a little solace in her garden, as once her brother had done.

Once again, autumn arrived and replete with all its golden legions. Lillian, standing silently, gave an involuntary shudder as a weeping willow, caught in the breeze, tenderly lashed her. Breathlessly, it intoned: "How my heart trembles at your vanished presence." Only nature punctuated her endless emptiness, yet nature also denied her. If only she knew where Sebastian's lonely wandering had taken him.

Far away, over purple-black desolate moors and mountains; lakes smooth and black as ink; over ancient forests, as wild and old as time, strode a figure as desolate as the landscape of which he stood a part.

Through the early morning mist, the young man made his way through the dense bracken and fern that clung to his feet. In the distance, a forest threw out wraith-like shapes that shimmered in the rising sun. Was there really something awful within those sylvan glades? Something lurking, waiting to take him away from everything he had ever known, or ever loved: something to cast him into the eternal night?

His path led to the deep, dense foliage. Flecks of golden sunshine pierced the dying verdant canopy, turning silver in the rising diaphanous mist.

Absolute stillness made the wood eerie. One might have expected a birdsong - or even a whisper in the trees as the wind embraced them - but there was nothing. As quiet as the wood, Sebastian strode onward, pausing occasionally to stand. If only he had known that such still waters presaged an approaching storm: a storm that might well dash him upon rocks as jagged as the Welsh mountains.

As the trees began to thin, Sebastian found himself at the top of a hill, or rather, upon the peak of a vast expanse of land that looked down upon a valley. An old path, as broken and forgotten as those who had built it, spiralled down to a river, a bridge, and on the far side, a small village.

Sebastian made his way down the steep-sided, precipitous slope toward the village. Each footstep was a painful one, separating him from where he really wished to be.

As he approached the little stone bridge that spanned the fast-flowing river, the sun tore away its death mask and arose to bathe the land in what, Sebastian thought, felt like warm amber after the horrors of another sleepless night. Ghostlike and unreal, three figures, still in the distance but approaching, emerged from the rapidly vanishing mist. Half-glimpsed; ethereal.

Drawing nearer, their features became defined; distinct. A young man, perhaps twenty-five years of age, with a shock of red hair. A second man, perhaps twice the age of the first accompanied but whereas the first had been slim the second had a portlier frame that betrayed his age. He too had red hair, yet Sebastian's attention was drawn to a figure that walked between them.

In the fading mist, Sebastian almost thought the woman to be Lillian. Drawing nearer still, her eyes could be seen to be red and puffy. It also became increasingly apparent that, far from being with the pair by choice, her two companions held her in a firm embrace; one on each arm, apparently escorting her from the village. As the unlikely trio reached the far edge of the bridge, they came to an abrupt stop. By now, Sebastian was just a few yards from them.

Their halt had not been a simple stop, but also an abrupt turn that meant all three were now facing the right-hand wall of the little stone bridge. A few ill-constructed bricks were all that separated the three from the fast-flowing waters beneath them. Curiosity had got the better of Sebastian, but even he could scarcely believe it as the elder of the two men took a rope from his pocket and, pulling the woman's arms behind her, tied them roughly at the wrists. For her part, she now appeared compliant, even willing.

The younger of the two men produced a small, hessian sack. Drawing the woman's head toward him, it became apparent her head was to go inside. If the woman had been crying, she now accepted events with a calm, even dignified, resignation.

Sebastian had seen enough. His presence had seemingly gone unnoticed. Now it was time to make known his disapproval, putting an end to the perverse ritual. Drawing level with the three, he snatched the sacking and tossed it into the river, whereupon it sank and was lost from view.

"Eh, what are you doing?" The protestation was made to Sebastian's back.

"What are *you* doing?" Sebastian said as he spun around.

"Dad ...?" The younger of the two had turned, looking to his father to supply an answer.

"It's alright, son. Hey, you, leave us alone." The elder man sought to allay his son's fears, before turning to Sebastian.

Sebastian stood in glaring silence. Were they really going to throw a woman to a certain death, and speak of it as if he had interrupted a family day out?

"You, take your damned hands off her!" Sebastian pointed to the younger man. "Whilst you ..." For the first time, the elder man's eyes met with Sebastian's.

"But she's a whore. We throw whores in the river. It's what we do."

Despite trying to qualify himself, the elder man unhanded the woman and looked to Sebastian to make the next move. Sebastian looked for approval from the young woman. She really did look like Lillian, but that wasn't why he wished to help. Why should she suffer under some outdated feudal justice?

"You release her … now!" Sebastian brought his hand up and, with a pointed finger, thrust it to within a hair's breadth of the younger man's face.

"Do as he says, son." The father nodded an affirmation to his offspring, the younger man doing as he was told before, along with his father, shuffling away. Occasionally his head would turn around but, catching Sebastian's gaze, would quickly turn back. Only when the distance between them was deemed sufficiently safe did he feel brave enough to fire a parting shot.

"She's a slut." As he said it, he turned quickly away and ran, leaving his father to slowly follow.

As the two men faded into the distance, Sebastian's thoughts came back to his own situation and that of the still-unnamed woman. There was an awkwardness to their plight that he had not anticipated. Would she look to him for answers? She could not go back to her own village, obviously, for they would only succeed in what they had already attempted. She was now as much an outcast and a wanderer as he.

Sebastian turned to face the woman.

"Thank you. What do you mean to do with me?" Her voice was almost inaudible; pathetic. It appeared that no recourse other than victim had ever been open to her.

"I don't mean to do anything with you. You're free to go." Sebastian averted his eyes and looked at the river.

"Free to go where?" Freedom has its burdens: both she and Sebastian were free, yet neither had a place to call home.

"Well ... what's your name?" Sebastian said, letting out a sigh.

"Sabrina."

"Ah, Goddess of the Severn," Sebastian said before the irony of the name and her recent situation dawned on him. "Well, Sabrina, suppose I give you a little money. Is there a place to which you could then go?" Sebastian brought himself around to face the woman.

"I've no place to go. I wish you had let them drown me. I can't be with the person I love. I've no home. I wish I were dead." Sabrina sat down and rested her back against the wall of the bridge.

"I can understand that," Sebastian said, causing Sabrina to look at him with surprise.

"You can? Have you ever loved someone, then?" It wasn't that Sabrina was prying, simply that she had a naive curiosity more often associated with children.

"Yes. Yes, I have." Sabrina was intrigued by Sebastian's wistful look.

"Did she love you?"

"I would like to think that deep down she did, but I'm not right for her. Perhaps she should find someone else." Sebastian looked back to the river. In the morning light, the sun had sent out golden trails that flooded upon it, making it appear a resplendent pathway to distant and exotic lands.

"Then you don't love her anymore?"

"I love her more than life. Her happiness is my happiness."

"Nobody's ever loved me like that." Sabrina looked from Sebastian to the wall on the other side of the bridge, opposite.

"We must get away from here. They're bound to come back for you." Sebastian stretched out a hand to help Sabrina to her feet.

"Let them. I don't care." There was no petulance in Sabrina's voice, only despair.

"Sabrina, death is a precious thing. Don't waste it." In the distance, Sebastian could see a mob approaching.

Sebastian made up his mind not to risk another refusal, so bending over, he scooped up Sabrina's unhappy form and carried her. In what seemed like a moment, they were back under the safety and cover of the trees. The mist had finally lifted. From the forest, a path had now emerged. Sebastian let Sabrina gently to the ground. Exhausted, he fell to her side and rolled upon his back.

"I could have walked, you know, but thank you for saving me ... I don't know your name." Sabrina brushed the indignation from her clothes.

"Sebastian." Sebastian, still prone, stared up at the sky.

"Nobody has ever cared whether I lived, or died, before." Sebastian's gesture had struck an emotional response.

"I'm sure they have." Sebastian turned his head to face Sabrina.

"They haven't. I've no-one. I'm frightened."

"You needn't be frightened." Sebastian tried to believe his own words but winced at their hollowness. What could *he* do? It would be impossible for him to take Sabrina with him for he had no place to go himself. It would be difficult for her to find employment in this area as it was far too remote and barren. She would have to go to the borders or the coast. If she went south, maybe he could help her. He chose to ponder the matter before making any suggestions.

"What was going on in that village?" There was a little curiosity in him, regarding Sabrina's situation, but the question was to buy him some time to think of how best he could help her.

"It's not what you think. I'm not a slut. I worked for a wealthy landowner, as did the other two you saw with me. Because I was poor and had no family, he took advantage of me. One day, last week, his wife caught us together. As soon as she had the chance, she told those two to throw me in the river. They've done it before … to someone else." Sabrina began her story slowly and without emotion, but by the end of it had begun to cry.

"I'm very sorry." Sebastian had intended to pay scant attention to Sabrina's story, but as the pitiful tale unfolded, he began to take an interest. By the end, her plight felt almost as real to him as it did to her.

For the first time, he was able to give her the attention she deserved. She really *did* look like Lillian. Both had the same dark hair and eyes; the same sensuous mouth and full red lips. The difference was their attire: whereas Lillian could now afford nice clothes from London, Sabrina's clothes were made of dark and heavy fabrics that were torn and dirty. But it was her boots that made her truly pitiful. It wasn't that she was pathetic, it was that circumstances had brought her to such a level. Huge working boots, that made her legs look painfully thin. That anyone should be reduced to this, Sebastian thought.

"Sabrina, will you do something for me?" Sabrina looked at Sebastian, intrigued.

"That depends."

"If I give you some money, will you go south for me with a message?"

"What do you want me to say? Who do you want me to see?" Sabrina, although not suspicious, did not want to commit herself.

"Here." Sebastian rummaged in his coat pocket and pulled out a perfectly creased letter.

"May I read it?" Sebastian knew she would eventually do so, even if he said 'No' now.

"If you must." Sebastian moved on to his back

again, staring skyward.

"My dearest love." Sabrina began the letter, reading aloud in the manner of those unfamiliar with such a practice. "I have never ceased nor can cease to feel for a moment that perfect and boundless attachment which bound me and binds me to you - which renders me utterly incapable of real love for any other human being - for what could they be after you? They say absence destroys weak passions - and confirms strong ones - Alas! mine for you is the union of all passions or of all affections - has strengthened itself but will destroy me." Sabrina finished and fell silent.

"I'm glad I heard you reading it." Sebastian took the letter from Sabrina and tore it in two.

"Why? What did you do that for? It was a beautiful letter." Sabrina was shocked by the violence of Sebastian's actions, especially after reading such beautiful sentiments.

"Because, Sabrina, the wages of scorned love is baneful hate. Why should I write such a glowing missive to one who has cast me aside?"

Sabrina stared at Sebastian, uncomprehending.

"Do you still want me to take a message then?"

"Yes. I want you to go to the woman I love and tell her I had your sister drowned because she was incapable of keeping a true affection for me. Say whatever you wish. I want her to *hate* me with a passion."

"Are you sure? That's an awful thing to do -

142

cruel." No sooner had she said the final word, Sebastian interrupted.

"Cruel? Cruel! Don't talk to me of cruelty. That's why I want you to do it. I want her to hate me. I want her to curse me … *and* the day we met. May her unquiet spirit know as little rest as mine."

"You sound as though you hate her," Sabrina began to wonder what sort of a person Sebastian was.

"Perhaps it is best if we hate each other. Shadows of death would only blight the marriage bed. I want her to find someone who can love her as an equal. If she has any feelings for me then she will never be able to do that. Will you take that message for me?"

"Yes, I will, but I think you're making a mistake." There was a little hesitancy in Sabrina's voice, before she agreed, remembering the debt of gratitude she owed the troubled man in front of her.

"Better to suffer the once, than be left to suffer for eternity … as I must," speaking the words under his breath.

"You talk as if you're immortal!" Sabrina gave a nervous giggle.

"Do I? I'm glad you find it amusing." Sebastian gave Sabrina a cold look, before averting his eyes.

"I'm sorry." Sabrina intoned, before falling silent. She felt embarrassed, now that Sebastian thought she had been mocking him. Even in the short time since they had met, she could see there was something painful deep within him: a wellspring of emptiness; of something unresolved.

"So, will you do it?" he said, before standing up.

"Yes, but I'm not happy at being the cause of so much grief." Sabrina had a rare sensitivity in her nature and genuinely cared for people. Like Sebastian, she would have given her life for love, or simply to have one person say they needed her.

"There will be a kindness in your cruelty." Sebastian may have had his doubts, but kept them hidden.

"I'm not convinced, but I will do it." Sebastian's face creased into a smile, which quickly vanished. He reached into his pocket and withdrew a card with Lillian's address upon it.

"Here's the address," he said, before passing the card to Sabrina.

"Aren't you coming with me?" Her voice betrayed her alarm.

"No. No, I cannot. I have my own path to follow. I shall give you a little money to help you. The town I want you to go to is a little more affluent than this one. You'll be able to get work there." Sebastian helped his companion to her feet.

"But what if I cannot?" Sabrina lowered her head.

"You will." Sebastian brought his eyes to focus upon the young woman who was looking to him to answer all her questions. Raising her eyes, they met with his.

"Do you promise?" Already, Sabrina believed him.

"You have my word." The words were hypnotic. Reaching inside a pocket, he pulled out a small reticule, which he then passed to Sabrina. Tenderly, he took her hand and, uncurling her fingers, placed the bag in her palm. The young woman stood staring at it.

"I can't. I can't take all this." It appeared as if she had never seen so much money.

"You can. If you do as I ask, I would pay you all I have." Sebastian spoke the words with assurance. "It's only money. We attach too much importance to it. All the money in the world can't buy the things that *really* matter. All material things eventually pass away."

Sabrina looked at him. She was a simple, untutored woman, yet her innately sympathetic nature went out to the man standing in front of her. She also knew of pain; of being a rare bloom, bruised and crushed by life. She may have been ill-educated but was as capable of as wide a spectrum of feeling as anyone.

The two made their way to one of the well-worn animal trails. Why hadn't Sebastian been able to find such a trail before? Within a short while, Sabrina caught hold of Sebastian's arm.

"Have you seen that?" Sebastian followed the direction in which she was pointing. At first, obscured by the dense undergrowth, it was difficult to make out to what Sabrina was pointing. Strange, unfamiliar, plants covered huge stones, but standing-stones carved and laid with purpose. The passage of time had made the ancient stones an anachronism, something that now had no place in a Christian country. What evil had so successfully burnt its own history, destroying the past? Sebastian knew but, for once, kept the answer to himself.

It wasn't long before the narrow track brought the two to the far side of the dense forest and back into the autumn sunshine. High in the sky, the flaming orb that had greeted the day a few hours before had turned pearlescent, yet still sought to spread itself over the desolate expanse in front of them. A single earthen track cleaved the landscape in two, it being the only thing that gave an indication that a human presence had, at some stage, sought to tame such a wilderness. Apart from that, the two might have been playing out a scene from any date in history. As far as the horizon, nothing could be seen save coarse grass, marshland, bracken, and fern. In the distance, an elevation in the land culminated in a mountain.

"Here we must part." Sebastian breathed the words as his eyes focussed on the horizon.

"I will be safe, won't I?"

Sebastian's heart softened. Had he never met Lillian, he might have found happiness with someone like Sabrina, but then she too, in time, would have had to know his dark and terrible secret. Even if he chose not to tell her, the inexorable march of time would have eventually betrayed him. The years would pass but his countenance would remain unchanged. Then, one day, in one way or another, she would be snatched from him and, once again, the terrible spectre of loneliness would descend leaving him alone for all eternity, to grieve for his lost love.

"Yes, quite safe." Sebastian turned his head to look at Sabrina.

"Then this is goodbye." Sabrina looked at Sebastian's for an indication otherwise.

"Yes, Sabrina. I'm sorry."

"So am I," Said Sabrina, gently pulling his head toward her own until her lips brushed the side of his face. Then she turned and, as casually as she could manage, gestured a last goodbye. Twice she turned to look upon his dark silhouette outlined against the trees. The third time she looked he was gone.

A few days later, Sabrina arrived in the small town, a town that had once been a camp for a Celtic tribe known as the Silures. Sabrina's appearance did not mark her out for undue attention so quietly and unobtrusively, the young woman wandered from shop to shop, buying a few things, yet all the while trying to muster the courage to perform her act of duplicity. More than once her nerves got the better of her and she thought of leaving, never to return. After all, Sebastian would never know, but then she thought about where she could go. There was also the obligation she felt to return Sebastian's kindness. She resolved to do what Sebastian had asked, concluding that he knew Lillian's mind far better than she did. If he thought that by telling her he had had a mistress drowned would spare Lillian's feelings then who was she to say otherwise?

She made her way through the old arch, and up the steep hill that separated the town from the outlying areas. Without expecting to, she quickly found herself on the right road. With trepidation, she made her way toward the large house that stood magnificent, overlooking the town. So much had changed so quickly. Had it only been a few days since she had lived and worked with people who, upon the words of an overlord, had suddenly tried to kill her? Those experiences felt like an empty lifetime ago.

She raised a small hand and, hoping no-one would answer, knocked on the old black door. A noise came from within as hard-heeled shoes hammered upon the flagstone floor. An unfastening of bolts preceded a fearful creak, as though some old tomb was about to give up its dead. The door finally opened and Gwen stood within the frame of the massive portal.

"Yes, can I help you?" Gwen smiled, her manner cheerful, which only made Sabrina's task all the more difficult.

"Miss Lillian? Do you know Mr Sebastian?" Sabrina had not waited for a response to her first question before asking the second. She felt embarrassed at not knowing either Lillian's surname or Sebastian's but felt it would be more mannerly to give them some sort of a title even if, after she had said it, she felt gauche. She had expected to stammer, or feel her face begin to burn; her nerves to unmask her as a fraud. Whilst thinking over her story, she had thought it a good idea to pretend she was estranged from her fictitious sister. It would be so much easier to play the role if little emotion was needed. She might be able to lie for Sebastian, but she couldn't act for him.

"No." Gwen's reply was emphatic.

"You don't?" Sabrina felt a rush of joy. The thought that Sebastian may have given her the wrong address, or that the family had moved, seemed like a blessing. After all, she had fulfilled her part of the deal.

"No, I'm not Miss Lillian. I'm her maid." Sabrina felt her optimism sink. She would have to carry through her awful charade after all. "I'll see if she's at home." Within a few minutes, Gwen had returned. "Come in."

Sabrina's heart began to beat a little faster, sending convulsions that the young woman felt in the back of her dry throat. The sides of her eyes began to pulse and darken. Gwen gestured for the stranger to follow her.

The two women walked a short way up one of the long, dark halls before pausing as they finally reached a door on the left. Gwen gave it a gentle knock. A voice from within indicated approval had been granted to enter. Gwen turned the handle, and the door groaned open.

"This is ...?" Gwen looked at the visitor with expectant eyes.

"Sabrina." Sabrina felt her long, dark hair

149

sticking to the sides of her face, burning it as though each strand were made of something incandescent.

"This is Sabrina." Gwen smiled and left.

For a few short seconds, Lillian said nothing. What did her guest know of Sebastian? It had been a long time since she had seen him; a long time since anyone had spoken his name. She imagined her lips saying his name. Delicious. Gwen's absence made the silence awkward

"Please, sit down. I'm forgetting my manners." Lillian gestured to a chair. "You have news of Sebastian?" Lillian's manner became officious. She had erected an emotional shield to hide behind; now someone had come seeking to knock it aside. It was unusual for Lillian to dispense with pleasantries, but passion affects us all in strange ways. As Sabrina sat, Lillian walked to the window, her back to her guest. She expected bad news, and something illogical within her made her feel that by not being able to see the bringer of ill-tidings then, somehow, the bad news would be lessened.

"Yes." Sabrina did her best to make herself comfortable in the soft, heavy chair but the whole situation left her feeling quite the opposite. She had become acutely aware of how her attire differed from Lillian's. Lillian had glided to the window like liquid and now stood like a classical statue. Her flowing cambric dress flowed with her. Short sleeves and a low neckline highlighted how clean the morning ablutions had left her. Sabrina looked at her own dirty hands and then at Lillian's shoes, shoes that were flat and pointed with a thin sole, cross-gartered in the classical fashion; as was the Attic grace with which she wore her hair. Even the room had a refined elegance to it that was far removed from the dark quarters of the near-medieval rustic retreat of other parts of the house. Again, Sabrina appraised herself. Her heavy working clothes jarred severely with those of Lillian. And what of her bare, unstockinged legs, terminating in a pair of oversized men's working boots, boots that had left a trail of damp mud on Lillian's carpet?

"Good or bad?" Lillian braced herself for the worse.

"Bad." Sabrina followed the word with a dry gulp.

"I thought as much." The dangerous liaison Lillian had had with Sebastian ought to have been tempered by her fear of him, but it was fear that made him so appealing. She had always expected he would somehow bring about his own undoing.

"What news have you?"

Now, Sabrina braced herself. She was glad that Lillian had turned her back on her as that made her promise to Sebastian that much easier to keep.

"Some time ago, my sister and I met Sebastian at a May Day Fair in our village. He introduced himself to us both but his interest, it soon became clear, was in my sister. It wasn't long before his attention was returned. I warned her because I could tell there was something odd about him. His passion for her was like a fire - often it appeared to be nothing more than grey embers, yet the slightest jealousy could cause it to burn with rage. Hers was a more constant flame that lit everything it touched. I could see that Sebastian cared less for my sister than she did for him, but she wouldn't listen. She never spoke to me again after I told her." Sabrina paused. By now she had warmed to her part, finding it easy to create a story from nothing. "Then one day, we heard she was expecting a child. I was told that he asked her to get rid of it - with a hot bath and gin - suspecting the child to have been fathered by another. She wouldn't. Somehow, he got a few of his acquaintances and - God save me - had her tied up and thrown in the river, for the infidelity he'd imagined. They fished out her body the next day."

For a long while, Lillian remained with her back to Sabrina. Silent tears clouded her eyes. She longed to turn and express her sympathies, but for who would those sympathies be? Sabrina and her sister? For Sebastian, and what he had become? For herself? If Sabrina's story were true - and she had no reason to doubt it - then Sebastian's embittered heart was lost to her forever. Eventually, she stemmed the flow of tears sufficiently to speak.

"I'm very sorry, but why bring me this story? What do *I* care of Sebastian?" Lillian did her best to sound indifferent but her voice had cracked as she spoke his name, doing her a disloyalty.

"It's the only address we had. He left in rather a hurry, leaving a few things behind. One was a letter with your name on ..."

"Where? Show me?" Lillian's quick and spirited interruption destroyed any pretence she had sought at indifference. She cared, and cared *too* much. Sabrina felt herself sink into her chair as remorse began to wash over her in an unholy ablution. She had raised the tearful young woman's hopes unduly. There was no letter, for no such events had ever taken place. Now, Lillian had turned to face her. Sabrina shifted uneasily in her seat, looking away.

"I'm ... I'm afraid I don't have it with me." Sabrina knew any inconsistencies in her story might unmask her as a liar.

"Did you read it? What did it say?" Lillian snapped the words voraciously.

"I'm afraid I don't read too well. Someone told me the address. My mother asked me to come and tell you, to see if you knew where Sebastian was." Sabrina let out a sigh. Lillian slumped into a nearby settee. How she wished she was small so that the folds of the fabric might have the expanse of huge fields, fields where she might lose herself.

The two women sat in silence. Lillian wishing to be alone; Sabrina wanting to leave, yet both lacked the words to bring their meeting to a close.

"Anyway, I'm sorry if it's all been a mistake. If you're not that close to him, I don't suppose any of this is of interest to you." Sabrina rose to her feet.

"I'm sorry about your sister." To speak any more of Sebastian would be too upsetting.

"Yes. May the gods have mercy on her." Sabrina looked anxiously at the door.

"I'll see you out." The conversation was becoming stilted; strained.

As the two walked the long hall, the only sound heard came from Sabrina's heavy boots. To little effect, she tried to walk on tiptoe.

Finally, they came to Lillian's front door. Quickly, Lillian opened it.

"Well, thank you for coming. I'm sorry I couldn't be more helpful." A strained smile flashed across Lillian's face.

"Thank you for listening. Goodbye", said Sabrina, escaping, Lillian closed the door behind her, without reply.

As the door shut, Lillian let out a sigh. Turning, she rested her back against the old timbers. In the dim passageway, it wasn't easy to see her whole body shaking, convulsing, as grief took its toll. Sobbing, she slid to the floor.

"Sebastian. Oh, Sebastian." The first call of his name seemed spoken to a friend: as if Sebastian had appeared in front of her. Her second intonation was softer, like the tone of a mother receiving a first birthday card from her child. Both times, sobs punctuated her phrasing.

Denial

Sebastian's scheme had failed. Lillian's affection for him had not dimmed nor lessened. In some strange way, she blamed herself for having driven him to such a base level; as though by spurning his affection, she had driven him to exact a terrible revenge upon all other members of the human race.

"Are you alright?" From the darkness, Gwen's voice came like a soft light.

"Dead. Dead." Through her veil of tears, Lillian murmured.

"Sebastian?" Although she had not met him, Gwen knew the name.

"Dead. Dead."

"Sebastian? Dead?" Gwen knew nothing of Sebastian's lonely and unending pilgrimage.

"Dead. Dead." Lillian began to wail uncontrollably.

Lillian closed her eyes. If only she were someone else; somewhere else. Somewhere where pain and misery would be unable to touch her. Yes, that would be nice. In the background, the perfect ticking of a grandfather clock stopped.

Sebastian's name was not often mentioned after that day. As the days turned to weeks, and then to months, his name was spoken less and less. Only Lillian remembered, when on the darkest nights the storms outside her window, and the rumble of thunder far away over the Welsh hills, reminded her of the night she had sent him away. The thought of him was never far away, but at certain times - when the whole universe appeared angry and tormented - the thought of him would become a constant one. Lying in her bed, sometimes it felt as though she could reach out and touch him, as he appeared silhouetted against the window. Running to meet him, her arms would pass through nothing more than cold shadows. She would open the curtains and, hope against hope, look out to see if, once again, his rain-soaked face might be there, gazing up at her from the garden far below.

Months became years. People came and went. Gwen married her hero. She continued to work for Lillian, despite having children and, in due course, her children having children. The Llewellyns had long gone the way of the flesh, as had Lillian's mother. Only Lillian sought to stay as she always had. She, however, was powerless to stop the years changing her. Now, when she looked in the mirror, she saw her once young and vibrant face turned into that of a lonely old woman, framed by silver hair, and with an expression bearing the saddest words of all: "It might have been."

Lillian was old. She had never married. How could she after *him*? Of course, she had had her chances. She had been both a beautiful and eligible young woman in her time but the days, like the suitors, were gone. How different things might have been if only she had been given the chance to change things. Now, it was too late. She had wasted a lifetime waiting. All those wasted years, years that might have been spent with someone who could have loved her as much as she loved him. It might have given her existence some meaning. Her happiness hinged on bringing happiness to others. It had all gone horribly wrong. This wasn't the way it was meant to have been. She had wanted a husband and children of her own.

As she closed her eyes, the wind and rain began to beat their familiar pattern upon the roof above her. Tapping the windowpane louder, it seemed, than usual. In the distance, thunder and lightning began to roll and crack, as though some ghostly coachman were whipping his nags, that they might draw their leaden load across the sky just that bit faster.

"Sebastian." The night, all those years before, when she had sent him away, came back to her waking dreams.

"Oh, Sebastian. I'm so sorry." Beneath her warm sheets, Lillian shuddered, remembering.

The tapping at the window continued. Lillian opened her eyes. As before, Sebastian's shape appeared, framed by the window, darkened by the tempest outside.

"Oh, Sebastian." Lillian knew the tricks her imagination played on her. This time, however, the image was more distinct than usual.

"Sebastian." She extended her arm. To touch his handsome face once again. "Sebastian."

"Lillian." The voice was clear and unique.

Lillian sat up, as quickly as age would allow.

"Sebastian?" Many times, she felt she had seen him, but never had he spoken - not since that fateful day.

"Lillian." The voice was soft and full of sorrow.

"Is it really you?" Lillian sought to contain her excited doubts,

"Oh, Lillian." The voice cracked with emotion.

"Come. Come to me." Lillian turned to light her bedside lamp. By the time she turned back. Sebastian had moved, yet remained hidden in the shadows.

"Lillian, I'm so sorry." His voice was grief-stricken.

"Come to me." Lillian still felt unsure her senses were being truthful. Slowly, Sebastian stepped into the light. "It is you! Exactly as I remember you!" Lillian realised what she had said. The years had passed, leaving. Sebastian unchanged. "Sebastian, I'm so sorry."

Sebastian pulled a chair to the bedside and took Lillian's hand in his. His still taut skin jarred against the wrinkled fingers they embraced.

"I loved you, Sebastian. I have always loved you." Lillian squeezed Sebastian's hand.

"But you sent me away." The years had not dimmed the anguish.

"I was young. It was a terrible mistake. I came after you but you had gone."

"Don't say it. Lillian, what have we done? I would gladly have spent those fleeting years with you and mourned you until the end of time if you had only said that you wanted to spend those years with me. It would have been worth it. I really thought you didn't want me."

"Because I was afraid. I was afraid of what other people might think. Afraid of my feelings for you. I was a fool. I denied myself a chance of happiness but I was young. I thought myself unlovable. When someone like you came along, I didn't know what to do." Tears made her eyes glisten before a few spilt out. Following the lines on her face, they trickled down to the pillow beneath her. "You're so young."

"It's a curse. I, alone, will have everyone I love taken from me, whilst I remain." Tragedy was in his voice.

"Sebastian, never forget. I shall *always* love you." Lillian gave his hand another squeeze and closed her eyes.

"I only ever wanted you to be happy. I wanted you to hate me so that you might find someone else. That you might find some happiness."

"But ..."

"I know what you're going to say. I sent her. She did it for me. I wanted you to hate me. I knew if you had any of the feelings for me that I have for you, you could never be free unless those feelings were shattered forever."

A smile played on the old woman's lips for a few seconds. Her gentle breathing became shallow. Sebastian brought Lillian's hand to his lips and pressed it to them. Another smile, then the breathing stopped.

Tears streaked their way down Sebastian's cheeks with a burning ferocity.

"No!" The cry was agonised and mournful. Tears rolled down his cheeks, and on to the hand still pressed in his. Running to the windows, he flung them open. From the balcony, he leapt to the garden below. The rain had turned to snow, turning hill and valley into an immaculate wasteland; featureless; unearthly.

To escape, Sebastian ran. Up to the bleak and barren Welsh moor. There, there was nothing: nothing except a white emptiness and an awful silence.

"Let me die!" Sebastian fell to his knees and raised a fist at the sky. "Let me die!" Falling forward, he buried his face in the snow. "Please, let me die."

Denied No More

Denied No More

But I have lived, and not lived in vain;
My mind may lose its force, my blood its fire,
And my frame perish even in conquering pain;
But there is that within me which shall tire
Torture and Time, and breathe when I expire.

Byron

For a long time after Lillian's death Sebastian stayed away from the old house. Shades still cast long shadows over his mind: to immerse himself in an environment where every memory that had ever mattered had taken place would have been too much to bear. The wandering continued. A fugitive and a vagabond upon the earth. Scorned, Sebastian remained a man of sorrows, well acquainted with grief.

Only after many months had elapsed did he feel able to return, all the while knowing that there would be no homecoming. No garlands strung from steeple to steeple would welcome the return of the errant brother.

As Sebastian trudged through the quiet streets, dark and abandoned as night began to fall memories came flooding back in a deluge. In the months since Lillian had died, grief without hope of respite had made him inconsolable. All those wasted years! Experience had twisted his heart until only the bitterest of dregs could now be wrung from it. Circumstances had denied him a chance for happiness. Some terrible knot of fate had conspired to waste not only his life but Lillian's as well: love would never flow through this world again. All that resided in his hard heart now was hate and a desire for implacable revenge. Others would suffer as he had suffered, he would make sure of that!

Well-worn paths led back to a familiar place. Looming large, the old house was nearing. Onward, through leafy glade and leafy bower. Beckoning, the house called to him like a siren on the rocks. Wearily,

Sebastian finally reached the outer reaches of the dark dominions of the old house. For a moment, it appeared unrecognisable. Before, there had always been a lifeblood flowing within it. Now, the house appeared exsanguinated and stood horribly alone. Every window had been boarded shut., reminding him of sightless eyes. Since the tragedy, the untended garden had grass that now stood waist-high. Rotting fruit lay on the ground, as did dead flowers.

Sebastian limped toward the house, as the last strains of a dying sun kissed goodbye to the old house's deathly facade.

For a short while, the old man stood in silent appraisal. Tearing aside a few boards, he pushed his way inside. Every piece of furniture remained as it was, only now, covered in the habiliments of the grave: death shrouds, motionless and funereal.

How life had altered in the years since Sebastian had first visited that house! Time had poured away. So much had changed: only he remained. Sebastian moved about the room. So much was still as it had always been. Furniture, ornaments, portraits, all as he remembered them. All awaiting the loving touch of a long-departed hand. How those few artefacts had shaped lives! Now, like lovelorn orphans, they awaited the return of she who had once needed them.

As he wandered further from the door, so the room became darker. The shuttered windows let in no light. Sebastian looked about him for a lamp or a few candles. In the gloom, a small candelabra presented itself. At last, there was a little illumination.

Tentatively, Sebastian stepped from one room to the next. He had not taken much notice of the rest of the house before, being more concerned about the people that had lived there. Now that all human life lay dead, there was nothing *but* the old house, however empty and lifeless it seemed.

Sebastian's boots echoed, as each footstep met with the cold floor of the long passageway. In the dreadful silence of the house, each retort seemed to reverberate throughout the entire building. Self-consciously, Sebastian tried to lighten his steps. Unknown to him, Sabrina had once felt the same, as she had walked the same corridor. That, however, had been more than half a century before.

Each door, as it yielded to Sebastian's caress, offered new surprises. Silently peering in, few brought back memories as he had never visited them, yet each one touched him; held him with the cold clasp of the past.

Finally, the corridor came to an end. The door in front led to a different wing, the wing where, many years previously, he had found all that remained of the white hart. Sebastian shuddered. He had no desire to go further or to venture upstairs. That had been where he had last seen ... No! Why *had* he come back? The question rolled about in his head like seawater in the hull of a sinking boat, lurching it from side to side, threatening to pull it beneath the waves. Maybe it was because the old house was the nearest thing he had ever come to a home; maybe it was to feel near those he had loved - and continued to love. He had hoped the old house would soften his heart, pouring a little compassion into that empty chamber, but even now, he was aware that it had not. Only anger, rage and impotent fury flowed within it. He who had created him had left him. She whom he had loved had spurned him. Worse still, he had once returned, only to find he had been mistaken, and that both he and Lillian had wasted a lonely lifetime. Now, nothing mattered. Now, there was nothing.

Sebastian made to turn back: to return along the corridor whence he had come. As he did so, something to his left ensnared his attention. There, in the half-darkness, a gilded mirror hung uncovered upon the wall. Sebastian approached with curiosity. How did others see him? Almost petrified, he looked at his own reflection. The mirror shimmered, returning the candle's tiny flame. A young-looking man gazed back, but more. In the gloom, his reflected features had become more than his own. A face was merging with his own, softening his masculine lineaments with a softer and more female aspect. Yet still, the face was his own: the countenance of his soul. For a moment - a fleeting moment - the face had been another's: Lillian's. Two *had* become one! Sebastian reached out a hand and touched the silvered surface. In that instant, the image was gone.

"Hey, what the hell are you doing in here?" Sebastian spun around as a gruff voice challenged him. At the far end of the corridor, an athletic-looking figure stood framed in the doorway.

"I lived here ... once." Sebastian was still shaken with the image in the mirror, his words now drifting like those in a dream.

"You never lived here, boy. My grandmother worked here as a maid for over fifty years. The only person that ever lived here was the woman she worked for." The words were spat with no intention of informing but in hostility. The figure began to approach.

"Then whose house is it now?" Sebastian shouted into the darkness,

"What's it to you? Get out!" By now, the figure had drawn close enough to face Sebastian. In the shallow light, he looked familiar. His lips, that sneer. What had he said? His 'grandmother had worked for the owner'. Sebastian knew where he had seen that face before. Gwen had married the man whom Sebastian had warned away from Lillian all those years ago. Not only had they had children, but their children had also had children. History had repeated itself.

Before Sebastian could reply, his arm was snatched and wrenched behind his back.

"Nobody's going to cheat me out of what's mine, got that?" The words were hissed into the side of Sebastian's face as he was pushed toward the door.

Sebastian's character had changed considerably

in the years between his encounter with Gwen's intended and the present encounter with her grandson. Hope had fled and mercy sighed farewell. Once there had been compassion in his heart, now there was none.

Sebastian allowed himself to be pushed toward the old back door. Breath tinged with the fumes of alcohol came from behind him. His arm suffered a tug as the figure behind him stumbled. Ah, once again, perhaps there was a way to capitalise on such a condition!

Finally, the two of them reached their destination.

"Wait! This house of yours. Care to take a little bet upon it? A game of chance? The rights to your inheritance, for all the money I have on me?" Sebastian's ploy had worked. They paused.

"And if I win?"

"As I said, I shall give you all the money I have, and you shall never see me again."

"And if I lose?"

"Then I will request you to sign something to the effect that you relinquish all claims to this property."

Sebastian felt the grip on his arm slacken.

"How much money do you have, then?" The words were spoken a little more quickly.

"Enough to buy this place twice over."

"I see. Then you'd better come back inside."

Sebastian smiled to himself, as he turned. In the darkness, Gwen's grandson lurched back into the room they had just left. He staggered about the room, lighting. a few candles, before sitting down at a table.

"I need a drink." Casting a glance about him, he pulled a hip flask from his pocket and took a large gulp.

"A game of skill, or a game of chance?" Sebastian had sat down at the same table. From an inside pocket, he had drawn a pack of cards.

"Chance." Gwen's grandson swallowed his drink and moved in his seat.

"Then we'll cut the deck. Highest card wins. Ace high."

Gwen's grandson nodded in agreement.

"You first?"

In the half-light. Sebastian leaned back in his chair, as his companion clutched at the deck before lifting his hand. The King of Diamonds. Even in the dim light, Sebastian saw his face break into a smile before his pursed lips blew a kiss at the heavens.

"C'mon, let's see your money." As if to emphasise his words, he banged the table with his outstretched finger.

Sebastian reached inside his coat pocket and withdrew a roll of banknotes of the highest currency and threw it onto the table.

"My turn." Sebastian reached out to the remaining cards and lifted half the pack. "Oh, bad luck! The Ace of Spades," Sebastian smiled and drew his wallet back to him.

"Wait! This house against *my* house." Gwen's

grandson was still looking dumbfounded at the deck of cards in front of him.

"Have you the deeds?"

"Yes, I have them on me. I've been to the solicitor today, to see about picking up the deeds to this place. I wanted to sell my home but had to prove I owned it. I have them here." He reached his hand into his pocket and, withdrawing it, threw the papers upon the table.

"Your house against this house?"

"Yes."

"That really doesn't seem fair. You wouldn't be trying to cheat me, would you? You and I both know this is the largest house in the area. Your house against the right to dispute whether this house is yours. If your case is a watertight one - and you feel confident - I'd accept that as a bet." Sebastian leaned back in his chair and smiled, awaiting a reply.

Gwen's grandson buried his face in his hands, before drawing them through his hair. Puffing out his cheeks, he let out a sigh.

"Yes, I suppose." Lifting his flask to his lips once more he took a second, larger draught. Downing it in one, he pulled a face as the liquid burned a fiery course to his stomach.

"Good." Sebastian reached for the deck of cards and shuffled them before placing them back on the table and withdrawing one.

"The Three of Hearts."

"Yes! Yes!" Gwen's grandson threw another kiss

at the gods. Slowly, he reached forward and lifted half the pack.

"Oh, what a shame! Two of Spades." There was little sincerity in Sebastian's sympathy. "I think I'd better find a pen for you to sign these deeds."

"I'm ruined. What of my family? I've no home. I needed this place. I have debts to pay." Gwen's grandson looked at Sebastian with plaintive eyes.

"Well, that really is a shame. I can see only one way out."

"What is it? I'll do anything." There was desperation in his voice.

"Kill yourself." By now, Sebastian had found a pen and thrust it into the young man's hand. It was taken, and the deeds duly signed.

"Oh God, what do I do know?"

"Leave *my* home for a start. And if you see your grandfather, give him my regards."

Early the next morning, Sebastian made his way into the little town nearby. Lillian had not told him who her executors were, but given that only one solicitor practised in the vicinity, Sebastian guessed there was a good chance any legalities might be in his hands.

The road into the town was a steep one. Houses crowded in on either side, reaching high, darkening the narrow streets below, even in the hours of daylight. Only when one passed through the ancient, fortified arch did the street pan out and become unusually wide. At the far end of the town, a castle imposed itself upon the fragile community, dominating the landscape as it had done for a thousand years. Beyond that, a river and cliffs presaged the onset of wild forests.

With intent, Sebastian made his way from the narrow, cobbled street that even in the early waking hours bustled with activity as the little community prepared for market day. Sebastian had no time for such matters. Circumstances were threatening to take him away from Lillian. He would kill to make sure that never happened again.

The sun crept over the town wall. How many generations had passed through that arch? How many had done so with as much purpose and meaning as he? What did it matter now? To what had all their plans come? All things must pass: nothing mattered.

As Sebastian pushed open the solicitors' office door, he glanced around in an effort to familiarise himself with the interior. It was an old building, rather dark and sombre. Panelled walls, stained, or perhaps dark with age, gave the inside a sinister aspect. Papers, some yellowed by time, were piled on every available space. It was then Sebastian became aware he was being watched. Two clerks, or perhaps the office junior and the solicitor, were exchanging nervous glances, both then looking with disdain at Sebastian.

"Can I help you, sir?" The eider of the two men lowered his spectacles as he spoke until they perched precipitously upon the end of his nose,

"Perhaps." Sebastian sensed the discomfort his

presence caused and revelled in it. Why should he offer them any respite? Slowly, and with mannered deliberation, he turned from the two, and walked around their premises, stopping at every picture to pay it some disinterested attention. Finally, he halted at the window where he remained with his back to the two.

"Sir?" A full five minutes had elapsed since the initial question had been asked. Sebastian turned his head and, looking at them, raised a questioning eyebrow. Eyes met momentarily. The solicitor again looked to his younger colleague. The elder man was, perhaps, sixty years of age. His receding hairline was swept back, revealing a full and rounded face. Broken veins upon his nose and cheeks suggested too fine an appreciation of port.

The younger of the two, all the while, remained silent. Unlike his senior, he had remained seated but enough of him could be seen above his desktop for Sebastian to take a guess at his position in the company. He was, perhaps, twenty-five years of age, yet still retained a shiny, inflamed complexion more often associated with a younger man. Unlike his superior, his hair was oiled, as was his moustache, and both were combed into perfect centre partings. Both men sported white shirts and dark waistcoats. Armbands, it might be supposed, sought to impress their clientele of their efficiency.

"A very close and dear friend of mine died some time ago. She owned the large house at the top of the hill." Sebastian folded his arms and brought one hand up to his chin.

"Yes sir, I'm aware of whom you mean. May I ask the nature of your enquiry?"

"She was without relatives. My enquiry, is to whom has the estate been left?" Sebastian slumped into a chair.

"Well, the will has been read. It was made rather a long time ago, I'm afraid. She left it all to a friend - a Mr Sebastian ..." he began, snapping his fingers as he looked to his junior to supply a surname. The younger man, taking his cue, began rummaging in a pile of papers.

"But", he continued, "we've been unable to trace him. There was a clause in the will that anticipated this. In the event of his not being found, the entire estate was to go to a friend of hers - a Miss Gwen ..." Again, the elder man looked to his minion to supply a surname, which only caused the younger man to rummage amongst the papers upon his desk even more furiously than before.

"In the event of her death - if I remember rightly - the house and all its contents were to go to her offspring, if she had any. Her grandson, I believe, survives, so barring us finding Mr Sebastian ..." furtive glances were again exchanged, "it would seem everything is to go to him."

"I see." Without explanation or even a departing grace, Sebastian sprang to his feet and left.

Conscious thought flooded through Sebastian's mind like a stream. If the will had been made fifty or sixty years ago, how would he be able to prove himself *the* Sebastian in question? The passing of years should have given him the appearance of an old man. He was old - very old - but looked, at most, to be a man of twenty-five. How would he be able to explain his apparent youth?

The rest of that day was spent in aimless wander, but unlike the hopeless meanderings of the past Sebastian was, this day, lost in a reverie. He longed to go back to the house, but to do so would merely confuse matters all the more. What to do? How could he prove he was the legitimate heir to Lillian's estate? There had to be some way.

By the time Sebastian finally returned to the old house it was late. Lost in thought, he lit the candle that had been used the day before and sat down. There *had* to be something that could help his claim, but what?

With slow deliberation, Sebastian walked from room to room. In the time since the house had last been a home, thick layers of dust had come to rest on all the furnishings. Without life, the house felt as cold as death. There could be no question of Sebastian ever not wanting to live there for it was a part of *her*. Until the end of time, nothing and no-one would come between them again.

Finally, every downstairs room had been investigated, all to no avail. Sebastian pulled his coat tightly around himself and fastened it at the narrow waist. There was only upstairs left: then he remembered the night, many years before, when he had ascended the same staircase; then, he had had a brother to accompany him; now, he was alone. Pale silver arrows from the night sky pierced the same window, falling upon a face unchanged in over half a century.

Lost in thought, Sebastian twisted a door handle and found himself in the one room he had wished to avoid: Lillian's. Quickly, he slammed the door shut. No, it was too soon. He could not yet bring himself to enter *those* quarters.

Strange faces: lost faces: faces now misread by the passing of time: Sebastian walked past the portraits of Lillian's ancestors that hung in abandoned suspension. Would he too, one day, become like them? Made ridiculous - even hideous - by the passing years; unable to change: fixed?

No, he had to go back to Lillian's room: there could be no avoiding it. With trepidation, he made his way back through the dark, dusty passages brushing aside cobwebs as he went. Taking the handle in his hand, before giving it a twist, closing his eyes as he did so. This time, the door shuddered open. Letting out a sigh borne of relief rather than lassitude, Sebastian entered.

The room was as he remembered it. The bed; the chair where he had sat; the dressing table where Lillian's brush and comb still lay in silent expectation.

Sebastian's eyes burned. Was there anything in that room that might help authenticate his claim? On the walls, a few paintings hung. With uneasy curiosity, Sebastian moved from one to the other. Then, for a moment, one image seemed half recognisable. There, hanging nailed and crucified, was a portrait of himself, accurate to the finest detail. Anyone could see it was unmistakably him. And the title? 'St. Sebastian'. So that was why arrows were shown piercing his heart! This was the evidence he needed! The final proof! What's more, it was signed by Lillian herself. Sebastian took the painting from its mount and carried it with him to the door, locking the door as he left. Moving downstairs, he awaited the first strains of the morning.

Later that day, Sebastian made his way back to the solicitors with the painting, which he had now wrapped.

When he opened the door, the same furtive glances greeted his arrival. This time, no pleasantries were offered, only raised eyebrows and an expectant look.

A few hours later, Sebastian left the little office a wealthy man. He had proven himself to be *the* Sebastian. Looks, needless to say, had been exchanged upon the disparity of a sixty-year-old will that bequeathed an entire estate to an apparently twenty-five-year-old man. Still, facts had been proven. The house was his!

Walking home, Sebastian allowed himself a smile, rare since the death of Lillian, not that they had ever been that frequent. Now, however, in the space of a few days, he had gone from owning no property to owning two.

Back at his home, Sebastian spent the rest of the day pulling the boarding off every window in the house, and deshrouding every item of furniture, Finally, every unwanted board and sheet was taken to the garden, piled into a heap, and set aflame. In the half-light, the flames gave a living hue to the desaturated colours of the house, seemingly bringing it back to life. The house would now be as Lillian would remember it! Moreover, as *he* remembered it.

Over the next few days, Sebastian acquainted himself with the rest of the house, excepting Lillian's room, telling himself that it would be a long time before he could ever enter *there* again. Although it had provided him with the proof he needed, there had been a high price to pay. Seeing Lillian's few, pitiful belongings still, silent and waiting had touched something unhealed. All he had now were memories and who can throw their arms around them? Lillian's bedroom door was locked.

The next day, as Sebastian prepared for a visit to the other property he now fortuitously owned, he was disturbed by a knock upon his front door. In irritation, he briskly trod the corridor that approached it, revelling in the noise each footstep made as it echoed throughout his house. Snatching the handle, he threw open the door. Outside, huddled together, stood a woman of about twenty-five years of age, and two children: a boy of around seven years of age; and a girl, perhaps a few years younger.

"Yes?" Sebastian frowned at his visitors.

"Sir." Almost as soon as she spoke, the woman began to cry, drawing her children nearer to her as she did so. "It's my husband. He's killed himself." The woman brought her hands to her face and wiped away her tears. The children, bewildered and uncomprehending, looked up at her.

"Well? What business is it of mine?" Sebastian glanced behind him to a clock. Already, he was late.

"He left a note. He says you have the deeds to our house."

"Have I? Ah, I see! Yes, I have, I'm afraid he lost them. Very sad, but what can I do? He would have taken all I had if he had won." Not a trace of sympathy or compassion tinged his voice. "As a matter of fact. I was just on my way to see you. We need to discuss your rent."

"That's why I've come to see you. We've no money. My husband was the only one that worked. We've no insurance either. Sir, I've *no* money to pay you any rent."

"I see." Sebastian paused and brought a hand to his face in contemplation. "You'd better come in," Sebastian extended a hand inside the house, gesturing the three past him, before closing the door. "This way." Sebastian made his way past the little group and walked toward a door that opened into the room that had once been Lillian's reception room. Again, he ushered the three inside, before he too entered, closing the door behind him.

"Please sit down." Sebastian nodded toward a sofa and the young woman made her way to it, taking her children with her. Sebastian walked to a window where he remained, his back to them.

"This puts me in quite a situation. You see, the house you live in *was* your house, but was lost, as I'm sure you're aware. The house is now mine. This entitles me to charge a rent or - should I wish to do so - sell. I gather you're not in a position to pay rent, so you can hardly be in a position to buy. Now, where does that leave me?" All the while, Sebastian spoke the words, he faced the window. The question was a near rhetorical one. Other than a few gentle sobs, there was no response.

"There are, however, a few options. Either you get a job, I have you evicted - in order that someone who *can* pay can take tenancy - or I offer you accommodation here, employed as my housekeeper. For no money, of course! I'm not going to put a roof over your head *and* pay for the privilege." Sebastian turned, to see how his offer had been received: the three figures sat huddled against one another.

"I can see no other option if I want to keep my family together." The words were whispered: desperate.

"Then we must make some arrangements.

Obviously, you won't, need your own furniture so you may sell that. The servants' quarters here are adequately furnished. If you'd like to come this way. I shall show them to you." Sebastian led the little troop to the wing of the house that had once been occupied by the Llewellyns.

"Here we are then. Not the most luxurious of rooms, I grant you, but it's this or the streets. I think you've made the right choice. I'm going into town to organise my affairs. Acquaint yourself with your quarters, if you like." Sebastian looked at the young woman opposite him. How empty she looked: as if her life had been taken from her, leaving only a shell behind. Still, what did he care? Who had ever shown *him* compassion?

Sebastian closed the door behind him and departed. How strange recent events had been! Until very recently, he had been a rootless vagabond, blown wherever the cruel elements took him. Now his bitter heart had shackled him to one place alone. That same bitter heart had made him a man of means and given him Lillian's ancestral home; another property that would provide a regular income; a housekeeper who needed the shelter he provided so desperately that she would work for no pay. If only her husband realised the dire straits in which he had left his family! Perhaps he had, and that was why he had killed himself. What, of the two children? Perhaps it was grief that had made them so strangely silent, or perhaps they were simply too young to appreciate their dramatic collapse in fortunes. They were not unattractive children, acquiring their looks from their mother, and not their brutish father. The little girl had her mother's complexion and hair, yet whilst the mother's eyes were dark and hazel, the daughter's eyes were of a deep blue. It was the boy who had troubled Sebastian a little more. Whilst he had been in his presence, he could not think why but now, in hindsight, the reason became apparent: he had the same disdainful look playing around his mouth that had cursed his family. His father had had it, as had his great-grandfather. Always there was the look of disgust; of ill-disguised contempt; of unslaked retribution.

Days turned to weeks. Some degree of routine had been established in the running of the house. Sebastian shut himself away in the upper reaches of his new home, sometimes for days at a time. Every night, Branwen (for that was her name) and her children would hear him pacing back and forth. When the countryside was still and quiet, every footstep made the house creak. Branwen would draw her children toward her, fearing the wrath of God, as the very heavens above appeared to shake. They all knew not to approach his room.

Weeks turned to months. Branwen and her children became accustomed to their new surroundings. Despite the gloom of their own quarters, much of the house was open to them, thus leaving them free to enjoy the more spacious and airy rooms of the gothic pile.

Branwen began to treat the house as her own. As the months wore on, Sebastian's forays from his lonely abode became a little more frequent. Initially, she had hated him: he, after all, had been responsible in no small measure for the death of her husband. She could not forget how callously he had treated her when first she had come to see him to explain her plight, Now, as time - the universal panacea - passed, she had come to see qualities in Sebastian that others had not. Her husband had been a spendthrift, a womaniser and a drunkard. His paternal lineage had, at one time, been a wealthy one; her husband had never forgotten the fact, and for all his life he had considered work to be beneath his social status. He had married beneath himself - God knows, he told her often enough. Yes, he *had* worked, but so much of his money had been squandered in pursuit of selfish pleasures. All they had ever had was their home, and he had been prepared to gamble even that! To who else might he have staked it? Only good fortune had found her a sanctuary with Sebastian. Sebastian had saved her from a loveless marriage *and* had put a roof over her head. Her new house had a nice garden in which her children could play, which was more than her previous house had had. Yes, perhaps Sebastian wasn't a *bad* person after all.

High in the uppermost reaches of the house, Sebastian sought to lock himself away. For a long while, grief had made him desolate. He had taken care of finances; the rent from Branwen's old home was simply pin money. His own home, despite his apparent lack of concern, was well cared for. Now? Now there was nothing. There was no one except Lillian, and she was dead. How he had loved her! Time, however, had taken her from him as he had known it would. All that remained, for a long while, he had hated. He had anticipated the numbness. Good or bad, he could not feel *anything* anymore.

As dawn banished the night's purple legions, Sebastian sought to shake the ennui that often overwhelmed him and, rising from his chaise longue, walked to the still-drawn curtains. He liked the room as it secluded him from the rest of the world. High in the uppermost floor of the house, when the door and windows were closed, he sought to banish all thoughts of the world from his mind. As he drew the curtains apart, the warm day caressed his face. Fresh air blew into the room, accompanied by the sweet refrain of birdsong. Then a sound, at first indistinct and half-forgotten: the sound of laughing children, playing in the garden far below. Sebastian could not see from where the laughter came as the window did not look out upon the garden, that being one of the reasons he had chosen the room. He had not been aware that the garden was even within earshot until now. Now, chuckling children caused a thawing. Oh, to be young again! Where had it all gone wrong? Oh, to be a child and full of joy and untainted optimism! To see the world as a friendly place, with long days and short nights. Now, distant laughter had unfrozen memories half-lost. Blissful laughter, laughter that might once have been Lillian's and his, if circumstances had not cleaved them in two. Down there, there were no rules, no conditions, only a joy and happiness found in one another's company. Children's laughter rose like larks ascending, the laughter of children that should have been Lillian's and his. Sebastian cursed himself. Why had he - and he alone - suffered the curse of immortality and been excluded from the chance of such happiness?

Slowly, Sebastian turned back into the room. It had always seemed a large room, running the length and breadth of the house. Now, it appeared vast and daunting. Perhaps Lillian had once found solace in that same room, away from everything. Sebastian walked to Lillian's piano. In a smaller room, it might have been a centrepiece. In the high attic, however, it appeared small and insignificant. The passing years had given Sebastian the opportunity to acquire many talents, more talents than can be accrued in a normal lifetime and, gently, his fingers touched the keys. He closed his eyes and let the music waft over him like an exotic perfume, lifting him away, far away over the wild Welsh countryside. There, Lillian was young, and they were together. The music was slow, melancholic, and had brought a wistful air to the warm day with memories bittersweet. Suddenly, the playing stopped; only chuckling children punctuated the silence. Sebastian arose, and slowly made for the door.

By the time he had reached the bottom of the stairs, Branwen had stopped her work, having seen his approach. Surprised, she stood in silent expectation.

"Are those your children in the garden?" Sebastian drew nearer to Branwen until she could almost feel the warmth of his body next to hers in the narrow passageway.

"Yes, they're only playing ... *please*." Branwen's entreaty was pitiful. For a moment, she had lifted her hands to stay Sebastian's departure but had thought better of it. She thought he had not noticed but, of course, he had. Did she really think him such a monster?

Sebastian made his way to the door, without reply. Branwen followed, stopping when the door was closed to her. What could she do? She was in no position to admonish Sebastian as he might well ask her to leave if she did so, and then where would she be? Her heart sank as the melodious joy evinced in her children's laughter stopped. Surprisingly, it soon started again, only now a little fainter: more distant. Branwen opened the door and quietly walked out. She had expected her children to have returned to her, if not crying, then at least subdued and downcast. Why were they still in such good spirits? She had been able to see them from the window all morning: they had been playing on the lawn, just in front of the house but now it was empty. Brushing a few long, thick curls of hair from her eyes, Branwen moved to the top of the broken steps that led to the rest of her children's personal Eden. Still, there was laughter unseen. Suddenly, Branwen made a start. There, far below her, on the lawn by the gate, Sebastian ran about the garden, with Rhiannon - her daughter - high upon his shoulders. In the sunlight, Rhiannon's dark blue eyes gleamed like sapphires. Whooping with laughter, her son – Ifan - made concerted efforts to pull his sister from Sebastian's back. Even Sebastian could not suppress a smile, yet even as Branwen watched, the scene was a strange one: one might have been forgiven for thinking it one of a father playing with his children, but there was something more than that; something intangible. For some reason, it seemed as though *three* innocents were playing.

        Branwen returned to her work. She enjoyed looking after the old house; in a way, she felt it to be hers. Now that Sebastian had shown a little affection to her children, perhaps she could finally put her life back together. Could he be the father-figure she had always wanted for them?

        An hour or so later, Branwen heard the back door click shut. Laughter still filled the summer day so, for a moment, she wondered which of the three had tired of their play. From the kitchen, she walked to the room into which the back door opened, just in time to see Sebastian.

        "Had fun with the children?" Branwen tried to make her tone as friendly as she could. She had originally come from further west, along the coast of Wales, thus her accent was different from those of the central valleys, or the south. She received no reply.

"Sebastian?" For quite a while, Sebastian had permitted her and her children the use of his 'given name', as he called it.

"Yes, but they're not *my* children, are they?" Sebastian said with sadness, before moving Branwen aside and bounding up the stairs to his sanctuary, three steps at a time.

Neither Branwen, Rhiannon or Ifan saw Sebastian for a while after that day. Only in the nights when, perhaps accidentally, he left his window open could they hear a few strains of some lilting nocturne played on a piano high above them, as though channelled through some ghostly chamber before it met their ears.

Despite their being forbidden to do so, it wasn't long before the children ventured upstairs. If Sebastian would not come to them, then they would go to Sebastian. Neither Rhiannon nor Ifan were frightened of Sebastian: their only reticence was that Branwen might discover where they had been. She had forbidden them to pay Sebastian a visit because Sebastian had not requested their company. He had given them a home in which to live; the least she could do was respect his privacy.

As the children mounted the stairs, the almost inaudible sound of a piano came to greet them. Each child nudged the other forward until finally, amidst nervous giggling and half-suppressed panic, Rhiannon tapped on Sebastian's door with her tiny hand. The piano playing stopped.

"Who is it?" Perhaps it had not been such a good idea after all.

"Sebastian, will you come out to play?" There followed a sound of approaching footsteps behind the door that elicited a few fearful glances between the two children. Run? The door clicked open. Sebastian glared down at them before his face creased into a broad smile.

"No, not today. You may come in for a little while though, if you wish." Sebastian turned and walked back into the room. A cool breeze blew through the open window, billowing his hair and loose white shirt. The door slammed,

"Why don't you come out? It's a lovely garden. Have you ever been all the way around it?" The little girl fell to an idle chatter as she walked about the room, running her hands over everything within her reach, but paying no real attention to anything. Ifan remained silent. He walked to the window and peered out, before looking at the clear blue sky above. Sebastian walked back to Lillian's piano and sat at the stool, facing out into the room. He crossed his legs. He had enjoyed the children's company that day in the garden as their friendships had been fresh and unconditional.

"Ours is the biggest garden in the world, and there are pixies, elves, and people that only we can see," said Rhiannon, pointing at Ifan.

Sebastian looked at the two children. Yes,

Rhiannon did look like her mother, for both had the same hair and large eyes, despite the disparity in colour, whereas Ifan's badly-cut hair gave him a look of careless abandon. Even the look on his face appeared to have softened.

"Why don't you come downstairs with us? It's a big house so you won't be in the way." Sebastian laughed. Evidently, Rhiannon had no idea how, or why, she had come to live in the old house.

"We'd all like you to." Ifan had come to Sebastian's side and placed a finger on a piano key which he tapped lightly until it hammered out a note. Looking at Sebastian, he apologised.

"It's quite alright. You haven't damaged it," Sebastian looked at the little boy in front of him. Would he have sought Sebastian's company so readily had he known him to be, at least partially, responsible for his father's death?

"Who's that?" Sebastian looked at Rhiannon who, by now, had also drawn alongside. He had no need to follow the direction of her outstretched finger for he knew where it pointed.

"That's Lillian," Sebastian had found a portrait of Lillian, not long after he had found the portrait of himself. It was unfinished, but unmistakably her, and Lillian as he remembered her: young, and in the bloom of life.

"Who's Lillian?" Rhiannon's questions were artless.

"Lillian used to live here and was someone that I loved very much." Sebastian followed the little girl's gaze until his eyes met with those of the portrait.

"Why did you love her?" Ifan's curiosity had, by now, been aroused and he too asked a question.

"Why?" Sebastian had never asked himself that question before and, for a moment, paused. "I'll tell you why, Ifan. It's because she was the only woman I have ever met who had a key to the chambers of my heart."

"Where is she now?" Sebastian looked at Rhiannon, whose curiosity already seemed to have wandered elsewhere. Sebastian's failure to reply appeared not to have been noticed and the question was not asked a second time.

"Rhiannon! Ifan!" In the distance, Branwen's voice sounded.

"I think your mother wants you." Sebastian ushered the children to the door and shut it behind them, before returning to the piano.

He looked up at Lillian's portrait. Had it hung in Lillian's room, he would not have removed it. No, this had been found - along with a few other artefacts - in an assortment of different rooms. He probably accorded it far more worth than Lillian had ever done, but now it was all that remained of what once had been.

A few days later, Rhiannon and Ifan paid another visit. It had rained heavily for the entire day, and the two children had become bored. Gently, they knocked at Sebastian's door.

"Come in." This time, Sebastian knew who it was who sought his company: the two children entered.

In the far corner of the room, crushed by a lassitude of which Rhiannon and Ifan could know nothing, Sebastian managed a smile to greet their arrival.

"And how are you, my two young friends?" He enjoyed their company. The two children chatted with Sebastian, and with one another before Rhiannon was once again taken with Lillian's portrait.

"She's the lady in the garden." Rhiannon looked to her brother, who simply shrugged his shoulders, before continuing his duel with an unseen musketeer.

"You saw her in the garden?" Sebastian felt as though he had been struck by a thunderbolt.

"Yes, but she looks sad in the garden. In the picture, she looks happy.

"I recognise the necklace," Ifan interjected, having emerged victorious from his fight to the death and now taking an interest in what his sister said.

"This necklace?" Sebastian stood up and walked to the piano. Opening a little box, he pulled forth an ornate silver chain, with a large, tear-shaped stone. Rhiannon nodded, whilst Ifan broke into a gap-toothed smile.

"Why is it here?" Rhiannon walked to Sebastian and stretched out her hand.

"Would you like to put it on?" Sebastian let the cool metal run between his fingers. "Here, let me put it on for you," Sebastian crouched down upon his knees, and clasped the necklace together, around Rhiannon's neck.

"Look, Ifan, I'm a princess!"

"Why is it here?" Ifan looked at Sebastian, ignoring his sister.

"Because they help to remind me of the person that once owned them."

"How do they do that?" Rhiannon had given up admiring her reflection in the room's large mirror and walked to Sebastian with a new question.

"I'll tell you, shall I?" The little girl nodded in affirmation to Sebastian's question. "Well, here I have a black onyx necklace. If I press the stone to my closed eyes, I can see happier times. Here is her tiger's eye brooch - that reminds me of her hair as the sun shone through it, making it shine so much that precious metals seemed to be woven around each and every strand. Her cornelian earrings remind me of fire - passion. A haematite necklace, as red as blood ..."

"Urg!" Rhiannon pulled a face; Sebastian smiled.

"Jade reminds me of the garden, where once we walked. The turquoise - the blue sky under which lives can be truly lived, or existed in lonely isolation. The lapis - the midnight-blue, shot with a thousand gold stars, reminds me of the night we said our last farewell. Pearls - of the tears shed. Opal - shadowed with the colour of wine. How love intoxicates! The sapphire - beloved of Saturn - my star, I think - if I have any. The emerald -

doesn't the green remind you of the mountains of Wales?" Sebastian pressed the stone against one of his closed eyes and turned his head to the window. Lost in thought, only silence interrupted the quiet and haunted realms of his imagination. Putting the stone back in its box, he snapped the lid shut. "Where is your mother?" Sebastian looked at the two children sitting in front of him: both stared up, in open-mouthed attentiveness.

"Getting ready for church," Ifan answered; Rhiannon continued to stare in mute confusion.

"Oh no! She doesn't go to church, does she?" Despite the many months since Branwen and her family had moved in, Sebastian had noticed very little of the day to day running of their lives: news of Branwen's Christianity had been a revelation. "Well, go and tell her 'God is dead'. No, wait until you're in church and then tell her as loudly as you can. Will you do that for me?" Both children nodded.

"Will you take this off for me?" Rhiannon gestured to the necklace that still hung around her neck. Sebastian removed it and watched as the two little figures left, before closing the door behind them.

Sebastian let the necklace slide between his fingers. Slowly, he walked back toward the piano, passing the mirror in which Rhiannon had admired herself. Unconsciously, he placed the necklace to his own throat as he gazed, not so much at his own reflection, but the reflection of the necklace. Only then did he notice the mirror's image of his hands: gone were the large, powerful hands of a man. Somehow, they had shifted shape into the slender and delicate hands of a woman. What of his face? Now that he looked, his masculine features had softened. For a moment, hadn't it been Lillian's face in the mirror, holding the necklace to her throat? Lillian as he remembered her; Lillian as she was in her portrait: young and beautiful. What *was* happening? Sebastian closed his eyes in spiral confusion. Pale shade? Ghostly imaginings? Opening his eyes, the reflection of a man looked back: his reflection. There was nothing else.

Sebastian's room became dark unusually early that day. Normally, to dispel the night terrors, he would light a few lamps. Today was different for he continued to sit in hopeless night. Alone, in contemplation, the silence was ruptured sometime later by a sharp retort upon the door.

"Come in." The door seemed to almost explode open on his command, its hinges sending it crashing into a wall.

"Sebastian, may God save your twisted soul." Branwen stood framed in the doorway, her long hair falling about her face, her eyes flashing in undisguised rage.

"Branwen!" Sebastian feigned surprise but knew the real reason for her fury.

"I'm grateful for your putting a roof over my family's head when we needed it, but I won't stand for you corrupting my children's minds with blasphemies."

"Ah." Sebastian smiled, as he rose to his feet. Languidly, he made his way to the piano. "Let me play you a little piece I've written; it's called 'Ave Satani'."

"Stop it! Please stop it. What sort of man are you?" Branwen entered the room and slammed the door behind her.

Sebastian sat down at the piano stool and hit a few dissonant chords.

"Will you listen to me? I'm very annoyed. The children shouting 'God is dead' in the middle of the sermon! Haven't we suffered enough? Must you bring the wrath of God down upon our heads as well? I suppose it's all just a cruel sport to you, isn't it? Is it?"

Sebastian gave a momentary laugh.

"I can't help it! My sympathies are with the Devil!" By now, he was teasing Branwen, whose rage only made him search for new provocations.

"What are you, to say such things? No wonder this house has no luck."

"I love the Devil! I love the Devil!" Sebastian stood up and moved toward Branwen, swaying like a cobra, and repeating the words and revelling in their impiety. Suddenly, a stinging retort caught the side of his face; Branwen had slapped him and was about to do so again.

Sebastian caught her hand in a firm embrace as Branwen sought to again strike Sebastian with her free hand before that was also caught. With all her strength, Branwen sought to free herself, pushing Sebastian backwards until he crashed into a wall. The momentum of the push and the suddenness of the stop caused her body to fall heavily into his. In an instant, the two were pressed against one another. Her anger spent, Branwen's eyes met Sebastian's before she lowered her gaze.

Branwen's eyelashes brushed Sebastian's cheek; her lips parted.

"I'm sorry, Branwen." Sebastian felt the warmth of his breath reflect off Branwen's cheek, echoing upon the nearness of her face. The words had been spoken quietly. Slowly, Branwen raised her eyelids until her gaze, once again, met his.

"Sebastian." Branwen's eyes, even in the dim light afforded by the little room, flushed a little darker as her pupils dilated. A little breath, as she had sounded his name, brushed his face. Closing his eyes, Sebastian brought his mouth toward Branwen's. In supplication, her lips parted a little wider, before she too closed her eyes. For just a moment lips met.

"No, I'm sorry." Sebastian released Branwen's hands from his and turned sharply away. Only the click as the door shut told him she had gone.

By the next day, Sebastian's spirits had lifted a little. The weather had brightened to such a degree that he opened his window to embrace the day. In the distance, the sound of laughing children shimmered in the warmth of the morning. Had Rhiannon and Ifan really seen Lillian in the garden, or had their vivid imaginations taken the haunting image in the portrait and transposed it into surroundings with which they were more familiar? There could only be one way to find out…

Sebastian made his way downstairs. As his heels echoed through the cavernous halls, a door opened: Branwen. had heard his approach.

"Sebastian. About yesterday." Nervously, she looked anywhere, save at him.

"Yes, I'm sorry Branwen. It's not you, but me." An awkward silence followed as both sought the words to say next. "Anyway, I'm off into the garden." Branwen smiled as Sebastian departed.

It wasn't long before Sebastian found the children_

"Sebastian!" Rhiannon ran toward him, throwing her arms around him as he stooped to greet her.

"Now, where do you see my friend - the woman in the painting?" Sebastian tried his best to phrase the question as nonchalantly as he could, yet a tinge of anxiety remained.

"There! There she is!" Ifan pointed past Sebastian, in the direction of the gate. Sebastian quickly turned, his movement restricted by Rhiannon's arms around his shoulders. For a single, fleeting moment, Lillian had been there. Sebastian stood fixed. The image had gone. Eventually, he turned back to Rhiannon.

"Do you speak to her?" He gestured with his

head toward where Lillian had been standing.

"Yes, but she doesn't answer. She doesn't even see us. All she says is 'I'm sorry'..."

"And then she cries." Ifan, having no wish to be excluded, concluded his sister's sentence.

"Cries?" Sebastian could cope with seeing Lillian if she were happy, but the thought of her restless wanderings being unhappy ones was too much to bear.

"Yes, and this morning she had a white deer with her. They went through there." Again, Ifan pointed toward the gate.

"Did she? I won't be a minute." Sebastian's steps sounded as he crossed the scorched brown grass and cracked earth, toward the gate. In an instant, he was in the dark wood. It was empty. Downcast, he returned to the children.

"How often have you seen her?" Sebastian sat down on the arid lawn. A golden scourge from a merciless azure empyrean oozed over them like lava.

"We see them every day." Rhiannon had lost interest, leaving Ifan behind to answer what she now thought were Sebastian's silly questions. This was the first Sebastian had heard of there being anyone other than Lillian in the garden, then he remembered the time Rhiannon had first ever mentioned seeing anyone and she had said "people".

"Yes, there's a man who looks after the garden - he's old with silver hair. There's another man who stands over by the gate - he looks ill. There are a few others, but we don't see them very often."

"Do any of them speak to you?"

"No. It's as if they can't hear us." Ifan was beginning to become bored with Sebastian's constant questioning; already he was looking elsewhere.

"Does your mother see them?"

"No! Don't tell her we told you. She shouts at us and tells us off saying we won't go to heaven if we lie, but we're not lying. You won't tell her, promise?"

"No, I won't tell her that you told me, I promise." Sebastian pulled himself to his feet and brushed the grass from his clothes. "Thank you, Ifan. Your secret is safe." Ifan grinned.

Back in the house, Sebastian soon found Branwen; she was cleaning the windows.

"Branwen, have you ever seen anyone in the garden?" Sebastian tried to make his tone as innocuous as possible.

"People? What people?" For a moment, she had stopped what she was doing, but that meant looking at Sebastian. Her humiliation came back to burn her, so she continued her self-appointed chore.

"Have you seen *any* people?"

"No. The children say they have, but they've vivid imaginations. I've been with them and they've actually pointed to where they say these people are, but there's nothing. It's only in their imagination. Why do you ask? Don't tell me *you've* seen them as well!" Branwen laughed. She hadn't ridiculed Sebastian, merely made light of a situation she found unbelievable. As if Sebastian would be able to see such figures! The idea was absurd

"I just wondered." Sebastian thought about passing the question off as a joke, in order to avoid lying, but Branwen's suspicions had not been raised so he let the matter drop. "I'm going back upstairs." With that, he was gone.

Once again, weeks turned to months. Sebastian chose not to visit the garden, as he once had. The thought of seeing Lillian inconsolable, knowing anything he said to alleviate her suffering would not be heard would be unbearable. The children continued to visit him just as often, though Sebastian chose not to mention Christianity to them again. He would wait until they were a little older, and then explain the drawbacks of a slave mentality. Finally, summer turned to autumn, with all its bittersweet memories.

One day, as Sebastian sat at his piano, a distant rumble of thunder interrupted his playing. As the irregular beating of the rain upon the window panes washed over his fluid playing, he stopped. Then, *that* day came back to him, with all its haunted legions. In the decades that had passed since that fateful day, as black as night, when Lillian had sent him away, Sebastian had not had a day pass when he had not thought of her reasons for doing so. Yes, he could now see why, but shouldn't love have conquered reason? And what of the tragedy that had blighted them both?

Knowing that she had wanted him but, leaving it too late, he had never known when knowing would have changed everything.

Sebastian closed the piano lid and brought himself to his. feet. Unaware of his movements, he began to pace the room. In the storm, the room had become gloomy: suffocating. Lightning cracked, irradiating everything with the blue tinge of death. For a moment, as it had flashed, he had caught his reflection in the mirror, Where the flowing locks of black hair? Where the billowing white shirt? In the mirror, only Lillian gazed back, smiling: young as he remembered her; attired in the fashions of half a century previous.

"Sebastian, death shall be yours. You've seven years."

"Lillian!" Sebastian leapt toward the mirror with outstretched arms, only to recoil, as his fingers collided with the cold glass, shattering the image so that the shards fell about his feet. "Oh Lillian, I'm sorry. I'm so, *so* sorry! Please come back … I love you." Sebastian fell to his knees amongst the broken, silvered pieces and frantically clutched at them. Blood began to drip from his hands, staining the broken remains, and the floorboards beneath. Something *was* changing as he had not bled before. Something was now binding him to the world of substance and human affairs. Uneasily, Sebastian knew exactly what that 'something' was: in the past, he had loved without motive; loved for the pleasure of loving and being loved. Initially, in seeking to hold on to the past, he had loved the possessions bequeathed him simply for their sentimental value. Now, with his finances dwindling, the hideous spectre of future poverty - and the unceasing worry that poverty brings - was making him all too human.

Months again turned to years. Sebastian's face had finally started to age as penury laid an increasingly cold and bony hand more heavily upon his shoulder. Sebastian's relationship with Branwen's children superficially strengthened. Rhiannon became the daughter he had never had yet, at times, his relationship with Ifan became strained. Ifan, being a little older than Rhiannon, remembered his father. He remembered how one day there had been Branwen, Rhiannon, his father and himself together, as a family, and living in the town; the next day, his father had gone, and those that remained had come to live at Sebastian's house. Often, he would ask himself what had happened to bring about such a collapse into the flames.

Sebastian sensed Ifan's changing attitude toward him. From the unconditional acceptance of a child, he had grown to ponder the circumstances of his family's downfall. How long could it be before both he and Rhiannon found out who had been responsible for their father's death? Maybe Branwen knew already, but what if even she had no idea? She had never apportioned blame if she had thought him guilty in some way. How could he tell her that it was he who had pushed her husband to suicide? Moreover, how long would it be before the passing years betrayed the terrible secret of his immortality? Now that he had started to age, would he slip more and more into decrepitude but still be denied the comfort of a release from the prison of flesh and bone that housed his mortal soul?

Sebastian's relationship with Branwen had found an uneasy comfort. For a long while after their brief encounter, there had been tension between them. Time had also changed it for Sebastian dulling it until, like a bloom denied water, it had withered. For Branwen, however, the affection had been tended and carefully nurtured. That one moment years before when, for just a moment, their lips had touched and her eyelashes had brushed his cheek had been a seed. That seed had fallen on fertile ground. Now its root wrapped itself around her, possessing her; all the while Sebastian remained as distant as a deity. Unattainable, he had become all the more attractive.

Year piled upon year. After seven years, Sebastian wondered where was the end he had been promised as he closed the lid of Lillian's jewellery box. It had been a long time since he had last left the house. The children no longer mentioned the figures in the garden; perhaps they no longer saw them. Now, Sebastian felt safe enough to venture outside, hoping Lillian had found peace at last. He could cope with seeing Llewelyn, or any other of the sad revenants that had ever been associated with the house. What he could not cope with was seeing Lillian, bewailing her loss, nor her brother, longingly staring at the gate with haunted eyes, his chest pierced with holes. As the days turned to weeks, weeks turned to months, and months turned to years he realised that time would never heal the anguished wounds branded upon his heart.

Sebastian made his way from his room passing Lillian's, by way of a change. Unconsciously, as he passed, Sebastian checked his pocket for her bedroom key. For seven years the room had remained locked. The key was still there, safe between his fingers. He smiled and moved on. In the kitchen, Branwen and her children were having a little breakfast. Ifan, now turned fourteen years old, had the stature of a man. The look of disdain that had occasionally played around his mouth had become noticeably pronounced. Rhiannon had turned twelve. Every day she came to look a little more like her mother, seemingly losing her individuality in the process. Continuity without change. Even Branwen had matured. She had once been an insecure young mother, a little unsure of herself and her place in the world. Once, life had seemed daunting, horrible, frightening. Then she had found God and happiness.

"Good morning, Sebastian," Branwen brought the teacup from her mouth and placed it back upon the table, before nervously brushing a few non-existent crumbs from her clothes.

"Sebastian!" Rhiannon, for the moment, still appeared enthusiastic at his unexpected arrival. Ifan remained silent, staring sullenly at the floor. Sebastian smiled at the assembled group.

"I'm going for a walk."

Branwen lifted her eyes and looked at Sebastian in astonishment. In the seven years she had lived at the old house, never once had Sebastian said he was venturing any further than the garden. Sebastian noticed the look Branwen had given him but let it pass without validating himself. Making his way to the door, he opened it wide and pushed aside the honeysuckle that cascaded in. Unbeknownst to Sebastian, Branwen had followed him.

"Off to see some friends, Sebastian?" Branwen's voice assailed him like the breeze that sways the long grass of summer meadows, cool and refreshing. For a moment, Sebastian paused before the horror of life came back to haunt him.

"Friends? Friends! My best friend would be he who would take a pistol and blow out my damned wretched brains." Before Branwen could respond, Sebastian was gone.

Branwen returned to the kitchen. Her children had gone to their rooms, leaving her alone. Why had Sebastian been so hostile? She had never done anything to hurt him yet, at times, he appeared to hate her.

In the garden, Sebastian slowly moved from one flower to another. He had always sought freedom but had seldom found it. Even in the garden, every perfume, every shimmering movement, every tender touch or sound seemed heavily laden with a memory.

Denied No More

Sebastian took a faltering footfall upon crumbling stone steps until, finally, he came to pause in an ancient rose garden. Every flower seemed to shiver in anticipation. Upon the ground, a few roses had somehow been torn from the rosebush that had lovingly nurtured them. Now dying, Sebastian wondered what hand had so cruelly torn away their life. Crouching, he picked them up.

"Oh Sebastian, I'm so sorry." The voice wafted light upon the air, echoing, as though whispered from some distant cavern. Quickly, he turned. Lillian stood at a short distance from him, imploring him to come to her. Behind her, a white hart nuzzled close.

"Lillian!" Sebastian ran forward. her with arms outstretched. There was no response or reaction for nothing remained. Lillian had been no more corporeal than a shadow. "No!" In the years since Sebastian had taken tenancy of the house, he had sought to avoid just such an experience. He had never wanted to see Lillian so woebegone and desolate, and being unable to alleviate her suffering made it even worse. They had reconciled their differences upon her deathbed, but that had obviously not been enough. Was this the legacy of a lifetime of suffering? No! It was too awful. Running, Sebastian made his way back to the house, throwing open the back door, and falling through it as if the portal were a pair of huge wooden arms to love and protect him; to console him in *his* sorrow. Sebastian slammed the door shut behind him.

"Are they for me?" He had quite forgotten the dying bouquet he still held in his hand. Now? Now there was Branwen's radiant face and voice as lyrical as a child opening its first birthday presents, looking at him with undisguised joy.

"What? These? Oh yes. Yes, these are for you." Sebastian extended his arm, keeping Branwen at a distance, all the while trying to regain his composure.

"Oh, Sebastian. You *do* care!" Branwen moved toward him, lifting her arms to envelop him.

"No!" Sebastian took a step backwards. Branwen's eyes reddened and became glassy; silent tears coursed her cheeks. "I'm sorry. Please don't cry." Sebastian felt acutely the pain of rejection. Then he thought of Lillian and how she must have thought when she had sent him away.

"How can I not?"

"I truly am sorry, but I just can't talk at the moment. I must go to my room." Sebastian manoeuvred Branwen aside and walked briskly down the corridor, before mounting the stairs in a few swift bounds. Once in his garret, he slumped against its door, sitting with his back pressed against it. Breathless, he closed his eyes. Within a few seconds, a knock came upon the heavy timbers behind him.

"Yes?" Sebastian found it hard to disguise the exasperation in his voice.

"Sebastian, I have to talk to you." It was Branwen.

"No, not now," Sebastian, having opened his eyes when Branwen had knocked, closed them again. Images of Lillian flickered across his mind.

"Sebastian, I must talk now." Branwen's broken phrasing told Sebastian she was crying. Slowly he rose to his feet and opened the door.

"May I come in?" Sebastian extended a hand, gesturing Branwen into the room. She entered, gently pulling Sebastian with her. "Sebastian, I can't keep the way I feel to myself any longer. Why do you treat me the way you do? You seem to hate me, yet you must have realised the way I feel about you." Branwen moved toward him. Clutching his forearm, she brought his hand to her warm mouth before pressing her red lips against his fingers.

"It's not you, Branwen. I don't hate you, but then I don't love you either." There was a pause, as Sebastian slowly pulled his hand away and walked toward the window.

"Branwen, I love another."

"Who? Who do you love? I've never seen you with anyone!" Branwen remained fixed to her spot: this time she had not followed Sebastian.

"I am near to her, however far away. I can never forget her: never lose her. You've not seen her because she's ... dead. You might ask why, then, do I still love her? I will tell you - because love knows neither life nor death. It is the one thing that survives us all."

"But I love you, and I'm here and I'm alive."

Branwen moved toward Sebastian, who, by now, had turned to face her. Drawing closer, she raised her hand and with the back of it, brushed his face. The effect could not have been more dramatic had she poured molten lead upon his bare skin.

"Please listen to me." Sebastian recoiled from the woman. His eyes flashed and his brow knitted.

"Sebastian, what is my crime? What have I done?"

"Nothing! Nothing! Nothing!"

"Then why do you treat me like this when my only crime is to care about you?" Branwen made no effort to stem her flow of tears. Sebastian turned away and paced about the room.

"How can you love me? You know nothing of me! Do you want to know the real me? The *real* me is the person responsible for your family's misfortune. I came to this house one night seven years ago, met your husband ... You don't understand. I *had* to have this house! Your husband told me the house was his. I suggested a bet, waging all I had with all he had. He lost. He begged me for help. I told him to kill himself. *That's* the sort of man I am! Now, tell me you love me. I didn't give a damn that he had a family. I wanted revenge. When you came to see me, no pity flowed in my heart. It wasn't charity that made me take you in. I needed someone to take care of the house, that was all. Don't you understand? I killed your husband, and took his home *and* family from him." Sebastian had no need to go on. Branwen raised her hands to her ears. Sobbing, she ran to the door pausing only to open it with fumbling fingers.

Sebastian breathed a sigh of relief and turned to face the window. He had thought of following Branwen, but checked himself: what else could he say? To console her would have been to undo the truth. To say anything further would have been superfluous; a cruelty. Now there was nothing, save himself and his catalogue of bitter reminiscences. How could he ever feel close to Lillian again? Perhaps there was a way.

Sebastian moved to the door, checking his waistcoat pocket to see if Lillian's bedroom key was still there.

With nervous trepidation, he unlocked Lillian's bedroom door. Years of dust had robbed the room of its colour so that everything now appeared to be in shades of grey.

Sebastian made his way about the room, laying his hands upon the precious things Lillian once might have touched. In the half-light of the darkened room, he looked pitiful, as though cruel nails had plucked out his eyes, yet however sightless those sockets appeared, they brought their owner to a sharp stop upon seeing Lillian's gilded mirror. In the gloom, another face appeared, reflected and smiling. Then a shape, indistinct at first, behind him.

Sebastian turned. Ifan's white fingers enclosed the handle of a carving knife. His knuckles white.

"Romans chapter twelve, five and nineteen. 'Vengeance is mine. I will repay, saith the Lord'." There was no emotion in the young man's voice as he approached.

"Ifan?" Sebastian took a few steps backwards until he could go no further, his back now pressed against the drawn curtains and the fragile leaded glass behind.

"No, Sebastian. John chapter eleven, line fifty. 'It is expedient that one man should die for the people'. It's too late, Sebastian. My mother has spoken to me. It's too late Sebastian. Too late."

The huge knife was raised high above the young man's head and, in one deft motion, brought down until only the handle remained visible, the blade piercing Sebastian's heart.

"Thank you, Ifan! Thank you!" Sebastian reached out to Ifan, speaking in a hoarse whisper. In trying to support himself, one hand had clutched the dusty curtain behind, tearing the ancient fabric away from its rails, bringing a cascade of dust down upon an ever-increasing expanse of blood beneath, blood flowed from Sebastian's chest and out upon the floor. Sunlight made it sparkle, like a string of rubies in a lead-lined casket. Suddenly, a gentle shape stepped from the mirror. With a loving touch, Lillian took Sebastian's hand, leading him back to whence she had come. Hands entwined. With soft and tender passion, Lillian pressed her lips to Sebastian's, raising her hand to bring his face nearer her own. Sebastian responded to Lillian's kiss with a slow and passionate kiss of his own.

"I love you, Sebastian. I've *always* loved you, and *will* always love you." Lillian spoke the words that both had always known, but which had been so hard to admit.

A soft breeze entered the room. Sebastian had broken a window when he had torn the curtains from the wall. Upon the floor, the warm summer air embraced Sebastian's long black locks, blowing a few strands across his lifeless lips. The morning sun caught the colour of his unblinking eyes. Outside, happy laughter, becoming distant, filled the garden.